I0764389

Tale of a Lantern
&
Other Stories

Publications from
The Scheherazade Foundation

The Secrets of Scheherazade
An Ordered Experience
Tale of a Lantern & Other Stories
The Elephant & The Tortoise & Other Stories
The Monkey's Fiddle & Other Stories
Ghost of the Violet Well & Other Stories
Many Wise Fools & Other Stories
The Frog Prince & Other Stories
The Three Lemons & Other Stories
The Twelve-Headed Griffin & Other Stories
The Antelope Boy & Other Stories
Why the Fish Laughed & Other Stories
Two Cats & Other Stories
Three Stories
The Twilight of the Gods & Other Stories
The Son of Seven Queens & Other Stories
The Moon Maiden & Other Stories
The Metamorphosis & Other Stories
The Celestial Sisters & Other Stories
Tales from the Arabian Nights I
East of the Sun, West of the Moon & Other Stories
The Well at the End of the World & Other Stories

Tale of a Lantern
&
Other Stories

Edited & Introduced by

TAHIR SHAH

The Scheherazade Foundation

The Scheherazade Foundation CIC
85 Great Portland Street
London
W1W 7LT
United Kingdom
www.SF.Charity
info@SF.Charity

First published by The Scheherazade Foundation CIC, 2023

TALE OF A LANTERN
& OTHER STORIES

Tale of a Lantern
Folklore From Tangier
Feridah Kirby Green
Folklore
1908

Knös
The Swedish Fairy Book
Clara Stroebe
Frederick A. Stokes Co.
1921

Doctor All-Wise
Folk-lore & Legends: Germany
Charles John Tibbitts
W. W. Gibbings Ltd.
1892

The Three Sillies
English Fairy Tales
Joseph Jacobs
G. P. Putnam's Sons
1892

The Yellow Dwarf
The Blue Fairy Book
Andrew Lang
Longmans, Green, & Co.

Geraint & Enid
Stories of King Arthur's Knights
Mary MacGregor
E. P. Dutton & Co.
1907

The King's Magic Drum
Folk Stories from Southern Nigeria
Elphinstone Dayrell
Longmans, Green & Co.
1910

The Boy Who Wanted More Cheese
Dutch Fairy Tales for Young Folks
William Elliot Griffis
Thomas Y. Crowell & Co.
1918

The Hare & the Lion
Zanzibar Tales
George W. Bateman
A.C. McClurg & Co.
1901

The Two Jugglers
A Chinese Wonder Book
Norman Hinsdale Pitman
E. P. Dutton & Co.
1919

The Princess of the Springs
Tales of Giants from Brazil
Elsie Spicer Eells
Dodd, Mead & Co.
1918

The Boy Who Set a Snare for the Sun
The Indian Fairy Book
Cornelius Mathews
Allen Brothers & Co.
1869

A CIP catalogue record for this title is available from the British Library.

ISBN 978-1-915311-12-2

Contents

Series Introduction

FROM EARLIEST CHILDHOOD, I was told stories.

Of course, I was – most children are told stories.

After all, telling children stories is one of the foundations that makes their early experiences a childhood.

But as I think back to the first years of my own life, I find myself reeling from the sheer quantity of stories my infant ears took in.

Whereas other children my age were told stories for amusement, my parents (and the people they associated with) recounted the endless streams of tales for a different reason.

In their opinion, stories – and the ability to tell them – were part of an ancient alchemy… a way of processing complex ideas, of solving problems, and of developing the human mind.

My father, the writer and thinker Idries Shah, believed that folklore was the single most important breakthrough ever developed by the human species. The way he saw it, the rise of stories was as consequential as the development of the languages in which they were told.

He would say that, without stories and storytelling, humanity would never have evolved in the way that it has – and that the folktales, which form a bedrock of ancient societies, are more precious than any physical artefact unearthed on an archaeological dig.

As the years of my own childhood slipped by, I found myself unbothered to work out the hidden layers within treasuries of stories – what my father called 'instruction manuals to the world'. Like everyone else, I simply absorbed the individual tales, delighting in them.

And that's it – the key point, the genius of stories and storytelling.

It's a thing I only grasped in adulthood… something that fascinates me deeply.

In the same way you can jump into a car and drive across the country without giving a second thought to the engine or how it works, you can appreciate stories without understanding the hidden layers and devices that make them what they are.

Stories are all around us.

They're in the TV and movies we so adore, in the video games we play, and of course in the books we read. They're in newspapers and magazines, too; in the conversations we share with old friends, and with new ones. They're on our mobile phones, in aeroplanes, in submarines, and even in our dreams.

Our obsession with, and craving for, stories rests squarely with the way we are so absorbed by them, just as it does with the way we don't need to continually consider how and why they work.

Throughout my life, I've devoted an increasing amount of time to gathering stories from all corners of the world.

SERIES INTRODUCTION

It began in my late teens, when I began to criss-cross the continents in a crazed preoccupation with folklore. I developed a first-hand love affair with societies that, over millennia, gave birth to their own astonishing traditions of stories and storytelling.

Most of the time, when reading or listening to stories, we forget that these tales have been shaped through the passage of time. Like pebbles in a river smoothed by rushing waters, they were honed through centuries of telling and retelling.

When I was twelve years old, my father published a masterwork, *World Tales*. The first edition was very large and featured hundreds of original illustrations. The book was unlike any that had come before, for it detailed the provenance and history of each story told.

At bedtime one night, he presented me with an advanced copy. For as long as I could remember, my father had been talking about the project.

Having an actual copy in my hands at last was thrilling beyond words.

Peering down at me sternly, my father said:

'This is far more than a book, Tahir Jan. It's the foundation stone of a great building… a building that *is* human culture. As you grow older, and as you go out into the world, you will understand that the folklores contained between the covers of *World Tales* have brought amusement and educated, and have solved problems when they were needed most of all.'

My father was right.

When I eventually headed out into the wilds of the world for the first time, I discovered the stories contained in *World Tales* for myself, along with a great many more. Just as he said, the stories published in his treasury were the warp and weft threads of society. Stories are the matrix on which culture itself is based – a framework that enables daily life to continue as smoothly as it does.

In this series of books, we have drawn together stories from all over the world. It's a mission begun decades ago by *World Tales*.

Some of the pieces will be known to you, and others will not.

Some will be easy to comprehend, while others will be challenging, or even nonsensical.

I'd now like to note something else…

The Occidental world seems to assume stories must appear in certain regimented ways – presented with a well-defined beginning, a middle, and an end. You know what I mean: the protagonist winning against all odds, and the happy ending to it all.

In the ancient tradition of teaching stories, the kind recounted for an eternity around campfires in the desert and in longhouses deep in the jungle, there's no such standardisation.

Rather, there's usually a hotchpotch of conflicting threads: stories without a straight linear narrative but with an underlying turbulence that gets the reader, or the listener, to sit up and think.

At The Scheherazade Foundation, we are preoccupied with the way we can extract knowledge from stories – either deliberately, or in a less structured way.

We hold the firm opinion that, in order to remove the marrow from the bone stories are best served up in the way as they were passed from one generation to the next throughout human history.

In this series, we have drawn together tales that were gathered in particular during the nineteenth and early twentieth centuries. Spanning a vast range of cultures, they offer an extraordinary glimpse into the societies from which they are drawn – societies that were often changed shortly afterwards by social upheaval, technologies, and war.

Indeed, the fact any of them were recorded at all is a thing of wonder.

Intriguingly, some of the tales will now appear dated because vocabulary and writing styles have altered. But the fact that they seem old-fashioned is of great interest – proof of the way stories are constantly changing and evolving from one era to the next.

Over the last thirty years, I've gathered hundreds of tales on my own journeys, most of them spoken directly into my ears by storytellers and fellow travellers, by wizened old men in the middle of nowhere, and by anyone else good enough to indulge my pleas.

On all those zigzagging adventures, one story sticks out, tantalising me whenever I turn it around my head.

It was called 'The Man Who Turned into a Cat'.

The reason I mention it here is not because it was an especially fine tale, but rather because, from that moment, it affected the way I perceive the world.

It was as though I were a lock and that, by hearing the tale, a key had been slipped into me and turned.

Since first receiving it, I've never been quite the same, my state of consciousness having been flipped inside out.

The fellow traveller who recounted 'The Man Who Turned into a Cat' was lost in shadow, no more than a fragment of his left cheek protruding shyly into the light.

We were sitting on low divans in a teahouse in the ancient Afghan city of Herat.

When the tale had been whispered, I sat there in silence for a long while.

'What have you done to me?' I asked after a long pause.

The fellow traveller offered half a smile.

'*I* didn't do anything,' he replied. 'It's the story that's affected you – a story that I myself first heard when I was a child playing in the orchards of Balkh.'

Peering into the shadow, my eyes widened.

'I don't understand,' I said feebly. 'After all, it's not an especially grand story. There wasn't even a jinn.'

The traveller's mouth eased out from the shadows.

Very slowly, it grinned.

'Tales containing the greatest sustenance for a soul speak in the softest voice,' he said.

Tahir Shah

Tale of a Lantern

THERE WAS ONCE a man, a rich merchant of Fez, who had a very beautiful wife to whom he was greatly devoted. He gave her all that her heart desired, and never allowed another woman to share her place in his life.

One day while they two were sitting over the evening meal, he drew from his bag a pair of very beautifully wrought silver bracelets and gave them to her, saying,

'See if these will fit your arms, beloved, for this afternoon my fellow merchants refused to buy them from the auctioneer, saying, "no woman had wrists small enough to slip them on," and I knew in my heart that my Fatumah would find them a world too large.'

And Fatumah, smiling, slipped the bracelets on with ease, for surely they fitted her as though they had been made to measure.

Then said Fatumah, 'Oh my lord, grant me one request.'

And he said, 'It is granted, on my head be it.'

And Fatumah said, 'Should it please the Almighty that I should die before my lord, will my lord promise that he will wed again she whom these bracelets, his munificent gift, will fit?'

And the merchant promised.

'Nay,' said she, 'but thou shalt swear, and Dada here shall be witness.' And he swore a solemn oath, and the old woman, who had been Fatumah's nurse, was witness.

And shortly after, it was decreed that Fatumah should give birth to a daughter, and die.

But the babe lived, and to it was given the name of Shumshen N'har, and the old Dada cared for her and brought her up, even as the daughters of Sultans are brought up. And she grew daily more beautiful so that she surpassed even the loveliness of her mother, and her father regarded her as the apple of his eye.

Now when Shumshen N'har had reached the age of fourteen, the relations and friends of her father spoke to him very seriously, saying,

'It is necessary that thou shouldst marry again. Behold your daughter is growing up and she ought to have a husband found for her, and who could arrange for her wedding so fittingly as her stepmother would? Wouldst thou leave such an important matter to the Dada? Moreover, when your daughter is married, your house will be empty and thou wilt require more than ever a wife to cherish thee and care for your welfare.'

And the merchant saw that they spoke the truth, and said, 'It is well. I will wed.'

That evening when the Dada stood before him to give an account of her stewardship that day and to hear his wishes, he told her what his friends' advice was, and that he had determined to follow it.

Then said the Dada, 'Has my lord forgotten the oath which he swore to the Lilla Fatumah, on whose soul be peace?'

And the merchant said, 'Nay, prepare thou the bracelets, so that when I hear of a suitable bride, thou mayest take them to her and see if they will fit her arms, and if they do, we will know that she is the wife Allah has destined for me, and if not, we will seek further.'

And the Dada kissed his hand and said, 'On my head be it.'

Soon after the merchant told the Dada, 'Go to the house of such a one. I hear he seeks a husband for his daughter. Maybe she is the one who will do for me.'

And the Dada went even as her lord commanded, but in vain. When the young girl tried to put the bracelets on, they stuck on her thumb bone, though she pushed until her hand was as white as milk. And thus it happened many times, so that the Dada grew weary of going from house to house with the bracelets; and all who saw them marvelled at their beauty, and at the smallness of the wrists for which they had been made.

And it came to pass that when the Dada returned from her tenth or twelfth essay, it was late in the evening, and she put down her cloak, and the handkerchief containing the bracelets in one corner of the kitchen while she hastened to prepare the evening meal.

And the Lilla Shumshen N'har entered the kitchen to speak with her and to help her. And she said,

'I will fold your cloak for thee, oh Dada, and put it away lest it gets soiled.'

And when she lifted the cloak, she saw the handkerchief knotted in a parcel. Then she said, 'Lo, what has Dada here?' and she opened the handkerchief, and when she saw the bracelets she admired them exceedingly and examined them carefully and then she tried them on, for she thought they must be a pair prepared for her by her father, and lo, the bracelets slipped on to her wrists and rested on her arms as though they had been made to her measure.

Then did Shumshen N'har clap her hands and call to her servant, saying, 'See, Dada, how beautiful these bracelets are, and how well they fit me. Did my father buy them for me?'

And the Dada came with haste and looked, and fell on the floor in a swoon, for she feared greatly.

And Shumshen N'har called the other maids, and they poured water on her face and rubbed her hands till she revived; but she would not tell them what ailed her, but groaned heavily, and then the voice of the master was heard, and Shumshen N'har ran to her own apartments with the bracelets forgotten on her arms, for she feared she knew not what. And that night, when the household was quiet, the Dada stood before her master and recounted to him what had befallen.

Then was that merchant greatly perplexed, and the next day he called all his chief friends and the learned men and the Kadi and laid all things before them. And for a long time they talked and wondered, and sought to find a way out of the difficulty, but they found none.

Then did the Kadi say to the merchant, 'Oh my son, seeing that thou hast sworn this solemn oath to your wife, on whose soul the Almighty have mercy, before witnesses that thou wilt marry the woman whom these bracelets will fit, and seeing that these bracelets fit only your daughter, Shumshen N'har, though thou hast tried them on other maidens, it seemeth unto me that thou must marry her. And if it does not please the All-Wise One to open a door of escape for thee before the wedding, thou canst but divorce her the day after the marriage ceremony and perchance thus thou may accomplish what is written in the Book of Fate.'

And the merchant bowed his head and agreed to what the Kadi said. And a wedding day was appointed, and the merchant went and lived in another house belonging unto him, leaving his former home to Shumshen N'har and the Dada, who set about preparing for the marriage, but with tears and lamentations as though she was preparing for a funeral.

As to Shumshen N'har, she shut herself into her own room and would see no one, and prayed day and night with tears that death might release her. And it came to pass one evening, that as the Dada was bargaining in the courtyard with a jeweller, about sundry ornaments of gold that he was preparing, that the moans of Shumshen N'har struck on his ear, and he inquired as to the reason of her grief, and the Dada recounted to him the story.

And the jeweller, being a charitable man, and having daughters of his own, was moved with pity for Shumshen N'har. And he said to the Dada, 'Verily, this is a sad tale thou hast related to me, oh my mistress. May it please the Almighty to interpose and avert the evil.'

And he said, 'Wallah, my tongue cleaveth to my throat with my wonder and pity. Give me, I pray, a drink of water to steady me before I go forth into the streets.'

And the Dada went away to seek a cup.

And whilst she was gone the jeweller whispered at the door of Shumshen N'har's room, 'Oh Lilla, fear not, I will aid thee, God willing.'

And she said, 'The blessing of Mulai Dris rest on you, oh charitable man.'

Then said the jeweller with haste, 'I will send a large lantern for thee to see. Hide yourself in it and I will get thee away from this place,' but before he could say more the Dada returned with the water. And the jeweller left, promising to send all the ornaments of gold with his apprentice so that the Dada might show them to her master before she paid for them.

And the next morning the apprentice of the jeweller came, and he brought with him a most beautiful lantern made of silver inlaid with gold, and coloured glass, and so large that it had to be carried by two men. And the apprentice said, 'My master has made this lantern for the son of the Sultan who is about to be wedded to the daughter of his uncle, Lilla Ameenah, and it is to be carried in front of the amareeyah. And my master has sent it for your master to see, so that if it pleaseth him such another may be made for his wedding.'

And the Dada said, 'Well, but my lord does not live here and I cannot carry this great lantern, as I can these jewels, from this house to where he lives, so that he may see it.'

And the apprentice said, 'Suffer it to remain here a little while, oh my mistress, for I have paid and dismissed the porters who brought it, and I will go quickly to my master and ask him whether he be willing that I should hire two other porters and carry it to where your master now dwells.'

And the Dada said, 'Well, but it is Friday and about eleven o'clock. If you go now, my lord will be at the Mosque. Come back this evening.'

And the boy replied, 'I will come back at Dehhor so that your lord may have time to see it and decide before sunset.' And he went off, leaving the lantern in the courtyard covered with a sheet.

And Shumshen N'har watched from the little window in her door till she saw that the Dada and the other women were busied elsewhere, and then she ran and entered into the lantern, seating herself among the candlesticks, and shutting the door after her. No sooner had she entered it when there came a knocking at the house door, and one of the slave children went to it. There was the jeweller himself and his apprentice and two porters, and the jeweller told how he had come to fetch away the lantern, for a message had come from the Sultan's house that it should be sent there immediately.

And the two porters lifted the lantern, and the jeweller was directing them how to carry it to his shop in the Mellah, when another messenger came from the Sultan's wife about the lantern, and he interposed, saying, 'Take it at once to the palace.'

'But, my lord,' said the jeweller, 'I have something yet to do to the door. At present it will not open or shut properly, so I have locked it, and the wife of our blessed Lord the Sultan will not be able to see the interior.'

'What matter, dog,' said the Sultan's slave rudely. 'Our Lady wishes to see it now, and as to the door, thou canst arrange it tomorrow or next day,' so the jeweller perforce let the lantern be carried into the palace with its precious burden.

By the time the porters arrived with the lantern, the Sultan's wife had lost all desire to see it, so the slave had it placed in a corner of the apartment of the Prince, for whose wedding it had been ordered, and left it there, still draped with its sheet.

Now the Prince, whose name was Abd-el-Kebir, had after the morning prayer gone for a long ride outside Fez, and returned to the palace late that evening, and so weary with his exertions that he ordered his people to bring him some supper into his room, and then to leave him to rest. And after partaking of the meal he threw himself on a couch and fell asleep.

Meanwhile Shumshen N'har had remained all day concealed in the lantern, scarce daring to breathe, until, overcome by weariness, she too slept. When she awoke it was about midnight, and she was consumed with hunger. Emboldened by the quiet that reigned around, she opened the door of the lantern and peeped out. She saw that she was in a lofty, spacious room, sumptuously furnished, and lit by a large lamp that hung in the centre of an arch. Beneath this lamp was a small table with a tray and food, and in the recess beyond, on a divan, lay a most beautiful youth fast asleep.

At first, overcome by fear and bashfulness, Shumshen N'har retreated back into her lantern, but her hunger was too much for her.

'After all,' said she, 'this youth seems too sound asleep to awake easily, and the food is not too near unto him. I will creep out, making less noise than a mouse, and assuage my hunger, and return ere ever he sees me.'

So she stole to the table side, and began eating with fear and trembling. But gradually curiosity made her creep closer to where he lay, so that she might the better see his features, and their beauty was such that she forgot all, but bent over closer and closer, and he, feeling that someone approached him, awoke suddenly.

At first these two glorious creatures gazed speechless at each other, and then with a cry Shumshen N'har strove to flee, but Mulai Abd-el-Kebir seized her caftan and implored her in earnest tones to fear naught, but to recount to him how it was that she was there. And his honeyed words prevailed on Shumshen N'har, so that her fear departed, and she told unto the Prince all her tale.

And Mulai Abd-el-Kebir comforted her, and made her eat food and rest on his divan, and he said, 'I will devise a way that thou escape from this dreadful thing that your people wish to do unto thee, and in the meanwhile thou shalt remain hidden in your lantern in this room, and none shall know that thou art here till I can find some other place where thou wilt be safe.'

And Shumshen N'har and the Prince talked together till the morning light peeped in at the window. And then she returned into her lantern and lay on some cushions he had placed there, and Mulai Abd-el-Kebir called his slaves and said, 'Let no one enter this room whilst I am out, and this evening place food there even as ye did last night.'

And thus it happened for three days. Every evening when the palace was quiet, Shumshen N'har emerged from her lantern and ate with the Prince, and spent the whole night in converse with him. And the heart of Abd-el-Kebir was filled with love for her, for her beauty was great, and he swore unto her by a great oath that he would save her from her father, and that he would marry her, and in token he gave her his ring, which was a diamond set in silver. And Shumshen N'har loved him with a love greater even than that which he had for her.

And on the fourth day Prince Abd-el-Kebir went with his young men to hunt gazelle, and whilst he was away, his sister, the Lilla Heber, said to her favourite slave.

'Mesoda, I will go to my brother's apartments this morning, for the air there is cooler than in mine, and I know that he will not return till evening,' and Mesoda said, 'It is well,' and the two went to the door of Mulai Abd-el-Kebir's rooms.

And the slave that was stationed there endeavoured to stop them, saying, 'Sidna said none were to enter there,' but Mesoda chide him, saying, 'Knowest thou not that is his own sister, the Lilla Heber, who wishes to enter?' and the slave feared and let them pass.

And Lilla Heber was much pleased with her brother's room, for it was much cooler than in the woman's court, and the windows opened into a small court full of flowers, and from them one could see the roofs of all Fez. Moreover, the room was filled with beautiful and strange things, and the Lilla and Mesoda amused themselves examining them all.

And Mesoda lifted the sheet off the lantern, saying,

'Behold this splendid lantern, oh Lilla. It is for the wedding of your noble brother and the Lilla Ameenah.'

Lilla Heber replied, 'It is truly a magnificent thing, and how large it is. I believe I could enter it.'

And she strove to open it, and Mesoda helped her, and at last they managed to open it, and there lay on some cushions a lovely maiden asleep. And when Lilla Heber saw her, her anger was great and her jealousy was kindled, and she said to Mesoda, 'Roll this evil thing in a mattress and bear her forth to the baker's and have her burnt in the oven, saying the mattress is infested with lice.'

And Mesoda did as the Princess commanded, stuffing a handkerchief into Shumshen N'har's mouth, and she gave a piece of gold to the slave at the door so that he might not tell Mulai Abd-el-Kebir who had entered the rooms.

And Shumshen N'har, rolled in the mattress and bound about with cords, was taken to the chief oven, and the master thereof told to bake the bale thoroughly, so as to kill the vermin.

But, thanks be to God, the baker's wife saw the bale, and when her husband told her that it was from the Sultan's palace she said, 'I will examine it before we put it into the oven, for perhaps it may have gold or silk embroideries on it that may spoil with the heat, and also, perhaps, I may get rid of the vermin in some other manner.'

And when she cut the cords and the mattress fell open, there within lay neither gold nor silver, nor noisome insects, but a fair and slim young damsel with a face like the silver moon, and hair that covered her as though with a garment. And the baker's wife took her into her own room and gave her reviving drinks until she opened her eyes, and then Shumshen N'har told her all her tale, and the baker's wife recounted how the Lilla Heber's slaves had brought her to the oven in a mattress.

Then did the baker's wife consult with her husband, and they agreed to keep Shumshen N'har hidden from all people, and they clothed her in poor clothes, like unto their own daughter, whose name was Aisha, and Shumshen N'har lived with these good people and assisted them in their labours. And Aisha was never tired of hearing her adventures, and made Shumshen N'har show unto her the bracelets that had been the cause of all her woe, and she tried them on, and lo, they fitted her as if they had been made for her; for Aisha also was a pretty maid and graceful, though not fit to be compared with Shumshen N'har.

But the ring of Mulai Abd-el-Kebir, Shumshen N'har showed to no one, and of his promise to wed her she said naught; but in her heart she dwelt on these things, and when Aisha and her parents slept, she lay awake and wept, and thought on the beauty and goodness of Mulai Abd-el-Kebir, and prayed to Allah and our patron Mulai Drees to keep him from all ill and to restore her to him.

Meanwhile, in the palace of the Sultan reigned woe and sorrow and distress, for Mulai Abd-el-Kebir, the favourite of the Ruler, had fallen sick, and shut himself up in his rooms, and would see no one and would eat no food, but lamented day and night. And no one knew the cause of his suffering. And his mother and his father rose up to comfort him, but he would have none of them.

And his sister, Lilla Heber, said,

'Let be, when he is wed with his cousin Ameenah, all will be cured,' and she advised her mother to have the wedding accomplished.

But when the Lila's words were repeated to Mulai Abd-el-Kebir he cursed her most dreadfully, and he swore that he would never wed with Lilla Ameenah, no, not if all women died and only she were left.

And the Sultan was greatly perplexed. But the Sultan's wife, she who was mother to Abd-el-Kebir, said, 'What matter this talk of brides and weddings? If my son eat not, he will die,' and she caused it to be cried through the streets of Fez that all women versed in cookery might prepare a dish of food which would be taken before the Prince, Mulai Abd-el-Kebir, so that peradventure he might be tempted to partake of one, and thus eat and live. Moreover, the wife of the Sultan promised a rich reward to her whose cookery would tempt her beloved son to eat.

And on the first day, many dishes were brought to the rooms of Mulai Abdel-Kebir, and he glanced at them, but with loathing, and would not touch so much as a grain of kuskusoo. And the second day it happened thus. And that evening the baker recounted to his wife how the Prince had fallen ill and how all the women of Fez were vying with each other to make delicacies for him, so that his oven, yea, and every other oven, were filled with delicacies.

And Shumshen N'har heard what he said, and when he had returned to his oven she said to his wife, 'Oh my mother, let me try also whether I can tempt the Prince to eat.'

And she got couscous, and some fat chickens and onions and vegetable marrows and spices and eggs and dates and raisins, and many other things. And she made a most succulent dish of couscous, and the outside she ornamented most lavishly, and on it, she wrote 'Bismillah' and 'Long life to our Lord' in cinnamon, and under that, she wrote the word 'Shumshen N'har,' and inside the couscous, right in the middle, she hid the diamond ring.

And it came to pass, that on the third day as the slaves passed before the couch of Abd-el-Kebir, carrying the various dishes that he might see them, that he caught sight of the couscous that Shumshen N'har had prepared, and he read what she had written thereon, and he beckoned to the slave who carried it to set it before him. And the Prince sat up and plunged his hand into the dish, and he felt the ring and he drew forth his hand and ate.

And then he said, 'Verily, this is good couscous. Find out who brought it.'

And they said, 'My Lord, my Lord's baker brought it and his daughter cooked it.'

And Lilla Heber's slave Mesoda was standing by, and she heard and trembled and fled unto her mistress. And Mulai Abd-el-Kebir arose and mounted his horse and went down to the house where lived the baker.

And the baker's wife brought out Shumshen N'har veiled unto him, and she spoke to him, and he knew her voice. And she told him all that had befallen her, and how she had found a substitute to be her father's bride, even Aisha the baker's daughter, and Mulai Abd-el-Kebir took her home to the palace and married her with great rejoicings. And the lantern was carried before her amareeyah by two porters.

And Lilla Ameenah was wedded to Mulai Abd-el-Kebir's brother, Mulai Abd-el-Wahed, and Lilla Heber was sent by the Sultan to Tafilet as a wife for the governor thereof, and Mesoda her slave accompanied her.

And for the charitable jeweller, there was a rich recompense.

And Shumshen N'har's and Mulai Abd-el-Kebir's love was blessed by many children, and they lived for many years in prosperity and happiness.

From: Folklore from Tangier

Geraint & Enid

QUEEN GUINEVERE LAY idly in bed dreaming beautiful dreams. The sunny morning hours were slipping away, but she was so happy in dreamland, that she did not remember that her little maid had called her long ago.

But the Queen's dreams came to an end at last, and all at once she remembered that this was the morning she had promised to go to the hunt with King Arthur.

Even in the hunting field, the King was not quite happy if his beautiful Queen Guinevere were not there. This morning he had waited for her in vain, for in dreamland the Queen had forgotten all about the hunt.

'If I dress quickly, I shall not be very late,' thought the Queen, as she heard the far-off sound of the hunting horn. And she was so quick that in a very short time, she and her little waiting maid were out, and riding up to a grassy knoll. But the huntsmen were already far away.

'We will wait here to see them ride homewards,' said the Queen, and they drew up their horses to watch and listen.

They had not waited long, when they heard the sound of horse's hoofs, and turning round, the Queen saw Prince Geraint, one of Arthur's knights. He was unarmed, except that his sword hung at his side. He wore a suit of silk, with a purple sash around his waist, and at each end of the sash was a golden apple, which sparkled in the sunlight.

'You are late for the hunt, Prince Geraint,' said the Queen.

'Like you, I have come, not to join the hunt, but to see it pass,' said the Prince, bowing low to the beautiful Queen. And he asked to be allowed to wait with her and the little maid.

As they waited, three people, a lady, a knight and a dwarf, came out of the forest and rode slowly past. The knight had his helmet off, and the Queen saw that he looked young and bold.

'I cannot remember if he is one of Arthur's knights. I must know his name,' she said. And she sent her little maid to find out who the strange knight was.

But when the little maid asked the dwarf his master's name, the dwarf answered rudely that he would not tell her.

'Then I will ask your master himself,' said the maid.

But as she stepped towards the knight, the dwarf struck her with his whip, and the little maid, half-angry and half-frightened, hurried back to the Queen and told her how the dwarf had treated her.

Prince Geraint was angry when he heard how rude the dwarf had been to the Queen's little messenger, and said that he would go and find out the knight's name.

But the dwarf, by his master's orders, treated the Prince as rudely as he had treated the little maid. When Geraint felt the dwarf's whip strike his cheek, and saw the blood dropping onto his purple sash, he felt for the sword at his side. Then he remembered that while he was tall and strong, the dwarf was small and weak, and he scorned to touch him.

Going back to the Queen, Geraint told her that he had not been able to find out the knight's name either, 'but with your leave, I will follow him to his home, and compel him to ask your pardon,' said the Prince. And the Queen allowed him to follow the knight.

'When you come back, you will perhaps bring a bride with you,' said the Queen. 'If she be a great lady, or if she be only a beggar-maid, I will dress her in beautiful robes, and she shall stand among the fairest ladies of my court.'

'In three days I shall come back, if I am not slain in battle with the knight,' said Geraint. And he rode away, a little sorry not to hear the merry sound of the hunter's horn, and a little vexed that he had undertaken this strange adventure.

Through valleys and over hills Geraint followed the lady, the knight and the dwarf, till at last, in the evening, he saw them go through the narrow streets of a little town, and reach a white fortress. Into this fortress, the lady, the knight and the dwarf disappeared.

'I shall find the knight there tomorrow,' thought Geraint

'Now I must go to an inn for food and a bed,' for he was hungry and tired after his long ride.

But all the inns in the little town were full, and everyone seemed too busy to take any notice of the stranger.

'Why is there such a bustle in your town this evening?' asked Geraint, first of one person and then of another.

But they hurried past him, muttering, 'The Sparrow-hawk has his tournament here tomorrow.'

'The Sparrow-hawk! That is a strange name,' thought Geraint.

But he did not know that this was one of the names of the knight he had followed so far.

Soon Geraint reached a smithy, and he looked in and saw that the smith was busy sharpening swords and spears.

'I will go in and buy arms,' thought Geraint.

And because the smith saw that the stranger was dressed like a Prince, he stopped his work for a moment to speak to him.

'Arms?' he said, when Geraint told him what he wanted.

'There are no arms to spare, for the Sparrow-hawk holds his tournament here tomorrow.'

'The Sparrow-hawk again!' thought Geraint.

'I wonder who he can be.'

Then he turned to the smith again and said, 'Though you cannot give me arms, perhaps you can tell me where to find food and a bed.'

'The old Earl Yniol might give you shelter. He lives in that half-ruined castle across the bridge,' said the smith.

And he turned again to his work, muttering, 'Those who work for the Sparrow-hawk have no time to waste in talk.'

So Geraint rode wearily on across the bridge and reached the castle. The courtyard was quite empty and looked very dreary, for it was all overgrown with weeds and thistles. At the door of the half-ruined castle stood the old Earl.

'It is growing late. Will you not come in and rest,' said Earl Yniol, 'although the castle be bare, and the fare simple?'

And Geraint said he would like to stay there, for he was so hungry that the plainest food would seem a feast.

As he entered the castle, he heard someone singing. The song was so beautiful, and the voice was so pure and clear, that Geraint thought it was the sweetest song in all the world, and the old castle seemed less gloomy as he listened.

Then Earl Yniol led Geraint into a long low room, and this room was both dining room and kitchen.

The Earl's wife sat there, and she wore a dress that must have been very grand once, but now it was old.

Beside her stood her beautiful daughter, and she wore a faded silk gown, but Geraint thought he had never seen so fair a face.

'This is the maiden who sang the beautiful song,' he thought. 'If I can win her for my bride, she shall come back with me to Queen Guinevere. But the brightest silks the Queen can dress her in, will not make her look more fair than she does in this old gown,' he murmured to himself.

'Enid,' said the Earl, 'take the stranger's horse to the stable, and then go to the town and buy food for supper.'

Geraint did not like the beautiful girl to wait on him, and he got up eagerly to help her.

'We are poor and have no servants, but we cannot let our guest wait upon himself,' said the Earl proudly.

And Geraint had to sit down, while Enid took his horse to the stall, and went across the bridge to the little town to buy meat and cakes for supper.

And as the dining room was the kitchen too, Geraint could watch Enid as she cooked the food and set the table.

At first, it grieved him that she should work at all, but afterwards, he thought, 'She touches everything with such grace and gentleness, that the work grows beautiful under her white hands.'

And when supper was ready, Enid stood behind, and waited, and Geraint almost forgot that he was very hungry, as he took the dishes from her careful hands.

When supper was over, Geraint turned to the Earl. 'Who is this Sparrow-hawk of whom all the townspeople chatter? Yet if he should be the knight of the white fortress, do not tell me his real name. That I must find out for myself.'

And he told the Earl that he was Prince Geraint, and that he had come to punish the knight because he allowed his dwarf to be so rude to the Queen's messengers.

The Earl was glad when he heard his guest's name. 'I have often told Enid of your noble deeds and wonderful adventures,' he said, 'and when I stopped, she would call to me to go on. She loves to hear of the noble deeds of Arthur's knights. But now I will tell you about the Sparrow-hawk. He lives in the white fortress, and he is my nephew. He is a fierce and cruel man, and when I would not allow him to marry Enid, he hated me, and made the people believe I was unkind to him. He said I had stolen his father's money from him. And the people believed him,' said the Earl, 'and were full of rage against me. One evening, just before Enid's birthday, three years ago, they broke into our home, and turned us out, and took away all our treasures. Then the Sparrow-hawk built himself the white fortress for safety, but us he keeps in this old half-ruined castle.'

'Give me arms,' said Geraint, 'and I will fight this knight in tomorrow's tournament.'

'Arms I can give you,' said the Earl, 'though they are old and rusty; but you cannot fight tomorrow.'

And the Earl told Geraint that the Sparrow-hawk gave a prize at the tournament.

'But every knight who fights tomorrow must have a lady with him,' said the Earl, 'so that if he wins the prize in fair fight from the Sparrow-hawk, he may give it to her. But you have no lady to whom you could give the prize, so you will not be allowed to fight.'

'Let me fight as your beautiful Enid's knight,' said Geraint. 'And if I win the prize for her, let me marry her, for I love her more than anyone else in all the world.'

Then the Earl was pleased, for he knew that if the Prince took Enid away, she would go to a beautiful home. And though the old castle would be drearier than ever without her, he loved his fair daughter too well to wish to keep her there.

'Her mother will tell Enid to be at the tournament tomorrow,' said the Earl, 'if she be willing to have you as her knight.'

And Enid was willing. And when she slept that night, she dreamt of noble deeds and true knights, and always in her dream the face of each knight was like the face of Prince Geraint.

Early in the morning, Enid woke her mother, and together they went through the meadows to the place where the tournament was to be held.

And the Earl and Geraint followed, and the Prince wore the Earl's rusty arms, but in spite of these, everyone could see that he was a Prince.

A great many lords and ladies and all the townspeople came to see the tournament.

Then the Sparrow-hawk came to the front of the great crowd and asked if anyone claimed his prize. And he thought, 'No one here is brave enough to fight with me.'

But Geraint was brave, and he called out loudly, 'I claim the prize for the fairest lady in the field.' And he glanced at Enid in her faded silk dress.

Then, in a great rage, the Sparrow-hawk got ready for the fight with Enid's champion, and they fought so fiercely that three times they broke their spears. Then they got off their horses and fought with their swords. And the lords and ladies and all the townspeople marvelled that Geraint was still alive, for the Sparrow-hawk's sword flashed like lightning around the Prince's head.

But Geraint, because he was fighting for the Queen, and to win the gracious Enid for his bride, brought down his sword with all his strength on the Sparrow-hawk's helmet. The blow brought the knight to the ground, and Geraint put his foot on him and demanded his name.

And all the pride of the Sparrow-hawk was gone because Enid had seen his fall, and he quickly told Geraint his name was Edyrn.

'I will spare your life,' said Geraint, 'but you must go to the Queen and ask her to forgive you, and you must take the dwarf with you. And you must give back to Earl Yniol his earldom and all his treasures.'

Edyrn went to the Queen and she forgave him, and he stayed at the court and grew ashamed of his rough and cruel deeds. At last, he began to fight for King Arthur and lived ever after as a true knight.

When the tournament was over, Geraint took the prize to Enid, and asked her if she would be his bride, and go to the Queen's court with him the next day. And Enid was glad, and said she would go.

In the early morning, Enid lay thinking of her journey.

'I have only my faded silk dress to wear,' she sighed, and it seemed to her shabbier and more faded than ever, as it hung there in the morning light.

'If only I had a few days longer, I would weave myself a dress. I would weave it so delicately that when Geraint took me to the Queen, he would be proud of it,' she thought.

For in her heart, she was afraid that Geraint would be ashamed of the old faded silk when they reached the court.

And her thoughts wandered back to the evening before her birthday, three long years ago. She could never forget that evening, for it was then that their home had been sacked. Then she thought of the morning of that day when her mother had brought her a beautiful gift. It was a dress, made all of silk, with beautiful silk flowers woven into it. If only she could have worn that, but the robbers had taken it away.

But what had happened? Enid sat up and rubbed her eyes. For at that moment, her mother came into the room, and over her arm was the very dress Enid had been thinking of.

'The colours are as bright as ever,' said the mother, touching the silk softly. And she told Enid how last night their scattered treasures had been brought back, and how she had found the dress among them.

'I will wear it at once,' said Enid, a glad look in her eyes. And with loving hands, her mother helped her to put on the old birthday gift.

Downstairs the Earl was telling Geraint that last night the Sparrow-hawk had sent back all their treasures.

'Among them is one of Enid's beautiful dresses. At last, you will see her dressed as a Princess,' said the Earl gladly.

But Geraint remembered that he had first seen and loved Enid in the faded gown, and he thought, 'I will ask her to wear it again today for my sake.'

And Enid loved the Prince so dearly, that when she heard his wish, she took off the beautiful dress she had been so glad to wear, and went down to him in the old silk gown. And when Geraint saw Enid, the gladness in his face made her glad too, and she forgot all about the old dress.

All that day Queen Guinevere sat in a high tower and often glanced out of the window to look for Geraint and his bride. When she saw them riding along the white road, she went down to the gate herself to welcome them. And when the Queen had dressed Enid in soft and shining silk, all the court marvelled at her beauty.

But because Geraint had first seen and loved her in the old faded silk, Enid folded it up with care and put it away among the things she loved.

And a feast was made for the wedding day, and in great joy Geraint and Enid were married.

From: Stories of King Arthur's Knights

Knös

Once upon a time, there was a poor widow, who found an egg under a pile of brush as she was gathering kindling in the forest. She took it and placed it under a goose, and when the goose had hatched it, a little boy slipped out of the shell.

The widow had him baptized Knös, and such a lad was a rarity; for when no more than five years old he was grown, and taller than the tallest man. And he ate in proportion, for he would swallow a whole batch of bread at a single sitting, and at last, the poor widow had to go to the commissioners for the relief of the poor in order to get food for him. But the town authorities said she must apprentice the boy at a trade, for he was big enough and strong enough to earn his own keep.

So Knös was apprenticed to a smith for three years. For his pay he asked a suit of clothes and a sword each year: a sword of five hundredweights the first year, one of ten hundredweights the second year, and one of fifteen hundredweights the third year. But after he had been in the smithy only a few days, the smith was glad to give him all three suits and all three swords at once; for he smashed all his iron and steel to bits.

Knös received his suits and swords, went to a knight's estate, and hired himself out as a serving man. Once he was told to go to the forest to gather firewood with the rest of the men, but sat at the table eating long after the others had driven off and when he had at last satisfied his hunger and was ready to start, he saw the two young oxen he was to drive waiting for him. But he let them stand and went into the forest, seized the two largest trees growing there, tore them out by the roots, took one tree under each arm, and carried them back to the estate. And he got there long before the rest, for they had to chop down the trees, saw them up and load them on the carts.

On the following day, Knös had to thresh. First, he hunted up the largest stone he could find, and rolled it around on the grain, so that all the corn was loosened from the ears. Then he had to separate the grain from the chaff. So he made a hole in each side of the roof of the barn, and stood outside the barn and blew, and the chaff and straw flew out into the yard, and the corn remained lying in a heap on the floor. His master happened to come along, laid a ladder against the barn, climbed up and looked down into one of the holes. But Knös was still blowing, and the wind caught his master, and he fell down and was nearly killed on the stone pavement of the court.

'He's a dangerous fellow,' thought his master. It would be a good thing to be rid of him, otherwise, he might do away with all of them; and besides, he ate so that it was all one could do to keep him fed. So he called Knös in, and paid him his wages for the full year, on condition that he leave.

Knös agreed, but said he must first be decently provisioned for his journey.

So he was allowed to go into the storehouse himself, and there he hoisted a flitch of bacon on each shoulder, slid a batch of bread under each arm, and took leave. But his master loosed the vicious bull on him. Knös, however, grasped him by the horns and flung him over his shoulder, and thus he went off. Then he came to a thicket where he slaughtered the bull, roasted him and ate him together with a batch of bread. And when he had done this he had about taken the edge off his hunger.

Then he came to the king's court, where great sorrow reigned because, once upon a time, when the king was sailing out at sea, a sea troll had called up a terrible tempest, so that the ship was about to sink. In order to escape with his life, the king had to promise the sea troll to give him whatever first came his way when he reached shore. The king thought his hunting dog would be the first to come running to meet him, as usual; but instead, his three young daughters came rowing out to meet him in a boat. This filled the king with grief, and he vowed that whoever delivered his daughters should have one of them for a bride, whichever one he might choose. But the only man who seemed to want to earn the reward was a tailor, named Red Peter.

Knös was given a place at the king's court, and his duty was to help the cook. But he asked to be let off on the day the troll was to come and carry away the oldest princess, and they were glad to let him go; for when he had to rinse the dishes he broke the king's vessels of gold and silver; and when he was told to bring firewood, he brought in a whole wagon-load at once, so that the doors flew from their hinges.

The princess stood on the seashore and wept and wrung her hands; for she could see what she had to expect. Nor did she have much confidence in Red Peter, who sat on a willow-stump, with a rusty old sabre in his hand. Then Knös came and tried to comfort the princess as well as he knew how, and asked her whether she would comb his hair. Yes, he might lay his head in her lap, and she combed his hair. Suddenly there was a dreadful roaring out at sea. It was the troll who was coming along, and he had five heads. Red Peter was so frightened that he rolled off his willow stump.

'Knös, is that you?' cried the troll.

'Yes,' said Knös.

'Haul me up on the shore!' said the troll.

'Pay out the cable!' said Knös.

Then he hauled the troll ashore, but he had his sword of five hundredweights at his side, and with it, he chopped off all five of the troll's heads, and the princess was free. But when Knös had gone off, Red Peter put his sabre to the breast of the princess and told her he would kill her unless she said he was her deliverer.

Then came the turn of the second princess. Once more Red Peter sat on the willow stump with his rusty sabre, and Knös asking to be let off for the day, went to the seashore and begged the princess to comb his hair, which she did. Then along came the troll, and this time he had ten heads.

'Knös, is that you?' asked the troll.

'Yes,' said Knös.

'Haul me ashore!' said the troll.

'Pay out the cable!' said Knös.

And this time Knös had his sword of ten hundredweights at his side, and he cut off all ten of the troll's heads. And so the second princess was freed. But Red Peter held his sabre at the princess' breast and forced her to say that he had delivered her.

Now it was the turn of the youngest princess. When it was time for the troll to come, Red Peter was sitting on his willow stump, and Knös came and begged the princess to comb his hair, and she did so. This time the troll had fifteen heads.

'Knös, is that you?' asked the troll.

'Yes,' said Knös.

'Haul me ashore!' said the troll.

'Pay out the cable,' said Knös.

Knös had his sword of fifteen hundredweights at his side, and with it he cut off all the troll's heads. But the fifteen hundredweights were half-an-ounce short, and the heads grew on again, and the troll took the princess, and carried her off with him.

One day as Knös was going along, he met a man carrying a church on his back.

'You are a strong man, you are!' said Knös.

'No, I am not strong,' said he, 'but Knös at the king's court, he is strong; for he can take steel and iron, and weld them together with his hands as though they were clay.'

'Well, I'm the man of whom you are speaking,' said Knös, 'come, let us travel together.'

And so they wandered on.

Then they met a man who carried a mountain of stone on his back.

'You are strong, you are!' said Knös.

'No, I'm not strong,' said the man with the mountain of stone, 'but Knös at the king's court, he is strong; for he can weld together steel and iron with his hands as though they were clay.'

'Well, I am that Knös, come let us travel together,' said Knös.

So all three of them travelled along together. Knös took them for a sea trip; but I think they had to leave the church and the hill of stone ashore. While they were sailing they grew thirsty and lay alongside an island, and there on the island stood a castle, to which they decided to go and ask for a drink. Now this was the very castle in which the troll lived.

First, the man with the church went, and when he entered the castle, there sat the troll with the princess on his lap, and she was very sad. He asked for something to drink.

'Help yourself, the goblet is on the table!' said the troll.

But he got nothing to drink, for though he could move the goblet from its place, he could not raise it.

Then the man with the hill of stone went into the castle and asked for a drink.

'Help yourself, the goblet is on the table!' said the troll. And he got nothing to drink either, for though he could move the goblet from its place, he could not raise it.

Then Knös himself went into the castle, and the princess was full of joy and leapt down from the troll's lap when she saw it was he. Knös asked for a drink.

'Help yourself,' said the troll, 'the goblet is on the table!'

And Knös took the goblet and emptied it at a single draught. Then he hit the troll across the head with the goblet, so that he rolled from the chair and died.

Knös took the princess back to the royal palace, and O, how happy everyone was! The other princesses recognized Knös again, for they had woven silk ribbons into his hair when they had combed it; but he could only marry one of the princesses, whichever one he preferred, so he chose the youngest. And when the king died, Knös inherited the kingdom.

As for Red Peter, he had to go into the nail-barrel.

And now you know all that I know.

From: The Swedish Fairy Book

The King's Magic Drum

Efriam Duke was an ancient king of Calabar. He was a peaceful man and did not like war. He had a wonderful drum, the property of which, when it was beaten, was always to provide plenty of good food and drink. So whenever any country declared war against him, he used to call all his enemies together and beat his drum; then to the surprise of everyone, instead of fighting the people found tables spread with all sorts of dishes, fish, foo-foo, palm oil chop, soup, cooked yams and ocros, and plenty of palm wine for everybody. In this way, he kept all the country quiet and sent his enemies away with full stomachs, and in a happy and contented frame of mind. There was only one drawback to possessing the drum, and that was, if the owner of the drum walked over any stick on the road or stepped over a fallen tree, all the food would immediately go bad, and three hundred Egbo men would appear with sticks and whips and beat the owner of the drum and all the invited guests very severely.

Efriam Duke was a rich man. He had many farms and hundreds of slaves, a large store of kernels on the beach, and many puncheons of palm oil. He also had fifty wives and many children. The wives were all fine women and healthy;

they were also good mothers, and all of them had plenty of children, which was good for the king's house.

Every few months the king used to issue invitations to all his subjects to come to a big feast, even the wild animals were invited; the elephants, hippopotami, leopards, bush cows, and antelopes used to come, for in those days there was no trouble, as they were friendly with man, and when they were at the feast they did not kill one another. All the people and the animals as well were envious of the king's drum and wanted to possess it, but the king would not part with it.

One morning Ikwor Edem, one of the king's wives, took her little daughter down to the spring to wash her, as she was covered with yaws, which are bad sores all over the body. The tortoise happened to be up a palm tree, just over the spring, cutting nuts for his midday meal; and while he was cutting, one of the nuts fell to the ground, just in front of the child. The little girl, seeing the good food, cried for it, and the mother, not knowing any better, picked up the palm nut and gave it to her daughter. Directly the tortoise saw this he climbed down the tree and asked the woman where his palm nut was. She replied that she had given it to her child to eat. Then the tortoise, who very much wanted the king's drum, thought he would make plenty palaver over this and force the king to give him the drum, so he said to the mother of the child –

'I am a poor man, and I climbed the tree to get food for myself and my family. Then you took my palm nut and gave it to your child. I shall tell the whole matter to the king, and see what he has to say when he hears that one of his wives has stolen my food,' for this, as everyone knows, is a very serious crime according to native custom.

Ikwor Edem then said to the tortoise – 'I saw your palm nut lying on the ground, and thinking it had fallen from the tree, I gave it to my little girl to eat, but I did not steal it. My husband the king is a rich man, and if you have any complaint to make against me or my child, I will take you before him.'

So when she had finished washing her daughter at the spring she took the tortoise to her husband and told him what had taken place. The king then asked the tortoise what he would accept as compensation for the loss of his palm nut, and offered him money, cloth, kernels or palm oil, all of which things the tortoise refused one after the other.

The king then said to the tortoise, 'What will you take? You may have anything you like.'

And the tortoise immediately pointed to the king's drum and said that it was the only thing he wanted.

In order to get rid of the tortoise the king said, 'Very well, take the drum,' but he never told the tortoise about the bad things that would happen to him if he stepped over a fallen tree, or walked over a stick on the road.

The tortoise was very glad at this, and carried the drum home in triumph to his wife, and said, 'I am now a rich man, and shall do no more work. Whenever I want food, all I have to do is to beat this drum, and food will immediately be brought to me, and plenty to drink.'

His wife and children were very pleased when they heard this and asked the tortoise to get food at once, as they were all hungry. This the tortoise was only too pleased to do, as he wished to show off his newly acquired wealth, and was also rather hungry himself, so he beat the drum in the same way as he had seen the king do when he wanted something to eat, and immediately plenty of food appeared, so they all sat down and made a great feast. The tortoise did this for three days, and everything went well; all his children got fat and had as much as they could possibly eat. He was therefore very proud of his drum, and in order to display his riches he sent invitations to the king and all the people and animals to come to a feast. When the people received their invitations they laughed, as they knew the tortoise was very poor, so very few attended the feast; but the king, knowing about the drum, came, and when the tortoise beat the drum, the food was brought as usual in great profusion, and all the people sat down and enjoyed their meal very much. They were much astonished that the poor tortoise should be able to entertain so many people and told all their friends what fine dishes had been placed before them, and that they had never had a better dinner. The people who had not gone were very sorry when they heard this, as a good feast, at somebody else's expense, is not provided every day. After the feast, all the people looked upon the tortoise as one of the richest men in the kingdom, and he was very much respected in consequence. No one, except the king, could understand how the poor tortoise could suddenly entertain so lavishly, but they all made up their minds that if the tortoise ever gave another feast, they would not refuse again.

When the tortoise had been in possession of the drum for a few weeks he became lazy and did no work, but went about the country boasting of his riches, and took to drinking too much. One day after he had been drinking a lot of palm wine at a distant farm, he started home carrying his drum; but having had too much to drink, he did not notice a stick in the path. He walked over the stick, and of course the magic was broken at once. But he did not know this, as nothing happened at the time, and eventually he arrived at his house very tired, and still not very well from having drunk too much. He threw the drum into a corner and went to sleep. When he woke up in the morning the tortoise began to feel hungry, and as his wife and children were calling out for food, he beat the drum; but instead of food being brought, the house was filled with Egbo men, who beat the tortoise, his wife and children, badly. At this the tortoise was very angry, and said to himself –'I asked everyone to a feast, but only a few came, and they had plenty to eat and drink. Now, when I want food for myself and my family, the Egbos come and beat me. Well, I will let the other people share the same fate, as I do not see why I and my family should be beaten when I have given a feast to all people.'

He therefore at once sent out invitations to all the men and animals to come to a big dinner the next day at three o'clock in the afternoon.

When the time arrived many people came, as they did not wish to lose the chance of a free meal a second time. Even the sick men, the lame, and the blind got their friends to lead them to the feast. When they had all arrived, with the exception of the king and his wives, who sent excuses, the tortoise beat his drum as usual, and then quickly hid himself under a bench, where he could not be seen. His wife and children he had sent away before the feast, as he knew what would surely happen. Directly he had beaten the drum three hundred Egbo men appeared with whips, and started flogging all the guests, who could not escape, as the doors had been fastened. The beating went on for two hours, and the people were so badly punished, that many of them had to be carried home on the backs of their friends. The leopard was the only one who escaped, as directly he saw the Egbo men arrive he knew that things were likely to be unpleasant, so he gave a big spring and jumped right out of the compound.

When the tortoise was satisfied with the beating the people had received he crept to the door and opened it. The people then ran away, and when the tortoise gave a certain tap on the drum all the Egbo men vanished. The people who had been beaten were so angry, and made so much palaver with the tortoise, that he made up his mind to return the drum to the king the next day. So in the morning the tortoise went to the king and brought the drum with him. He told the king that he was not satisfied with the drum, and wished to exchange it for something else; he did not mind so much what the king gave him so long as he got full value for the drum, and he was quite willing to accept a certain number of slaves, or a few farms, or their equivalent in cloth or rods.

The king, however, refused to do this; but as he was rather sorry for the tortoise, he said he would present him with a magic foo-foo tree, which would provide the tortoise and his family with food, provided he kept a certain condition. This the tortoise gladly consented to do. Now this foo-foo tree only bore fruit once a year, but every day it dropped foo-foo and soup on the ground. And the condition was, that the owner should gather sufficient food for the day, once, and not return again for more. The tortoise, when he had thanked the king for his generosity, went home to his wife and told her to bring her calabashes to the tree. She did so, and they gathered plenty of foo-foo and soup quite sufficient for the whole family for that day, and went back to their house very happy.

That night they all feasted and enjoyed themselves. But one of the sons, who was very greedy, thought to himself –'I wonder where my father gets all this good food from? I must ask him.'

So in the morning, he said to his father –'Tell me where do you get all this foo-foo and soup from?'

But his father refused to tell him, as his wife, who was a cunning woman, said – 'If we let our children know the secret of the foo-foo tree, some day when they are hungry, after we have got our daily supply, one of them may go to the tree and gather more, which will break the magic.'

But the envious son, being determined to get plenty of food for himself, decided to track his father to the place where he obtained the food. This was rather difficult to do, as the tortoise always went out alone, and took the greatest care to prevent anyone following him. The boy, however, soon thought of a plan and got a calabash with a long neck and a hole in the end. He filled the calabash with wood ashes, which he obtained from the fire, and then got a bag which his father always carried on his back when he went out to get food. In the bottom of the bag, the boy then made a small hole, and inserted the calabash with the neck downwards, so that when his father walked to the foo-foo tree he would leave a small trail of wood ashes behind him. Then when his father, having slung his bag over his back as usual, set out to get the daily supply of food, his greedy son followed the trail of the wood ashes, taking great care to hide himself and not to let his father perceive that he was being followed. At last, the tortoise arrived at the tree and placed his calabashes on the ground and collected the food for the day, the boy watching him from a distance. When his father had finished and went home the boy also returned, and having had a good meal, said nothing to his parents, but went to bed. The next morning, he got some of his brothers, and after his father had finished getting the daily supply, they went to the tree and collected much foo-foo and soup, and so broke the magic.

At daylight, the tortoise went to the tree as usual, but he could not find it, as during the night the whole bush had grown up, and the foo-foo tree was hidden from sight. There was nothing to be seen but a dense mass of prickly tie-tie palm. Then the tortoise at once knew that someone had broken the magic, and had gathered foo-foo from the tree twice in the same day; so he returned very sadly to his house and told his wife. He then called all his family together and told them what had happened, and asked them who had done this evil thing. They all denied having had anything to do with the tree, so the tortoise in despair brought all his family to the place where the foo-foo tree had been, but which was now all prickly tie-tie palm, and said –

'My dear wife and children, I have done all that I can for you, but you have broken my magic; you must therefore for the future live on the tie-tie palm.'

So they made their home underneath the prickly tree, and from that day you will always find tortoises living under the prickly tie-tie palm, as they have nowhere else to go to for food.

From: Folk Stories from Southern Nigeria

Doctor All-Wise

There was a poor peasant, named Crab, who once drove two oxen, with a load of wood, into the city, and there sold it for two dollars to a doctor. The doctor counted out the money to him as he sat at dinner, and the peasant, seeing how well he fared, yearned to live like him, and would needs be a doctor too. He stood a little while in thought, and at last asked if he could not become a doctor.

'Oh yes,' said the doctor, 'that may be easily managed. In the first place, you must purchase an A, B, C book, only taking care that it is one that has got in the front of it a picture of a cock crowing. Then sell your cart and oxen, and buy with the money clothes, and all the other things needful. Thirdly, and lastly, have a sign painted with the words, "I am Doctor All-Wise," and have it nailed up before the door of your house.'

The peasant did exactly as he had been told; and after he had doctored a little while, it chanced that a certain nobleman was robbed of a large sum of money. Someone told him that there lived in the village hard by a Doctor All-Wise, who was sure to be able to tell him where his money had gone. The nobleman at once ordered his carriage to be got ready and rode into the city, and having come to the doctor, asked him if he was Dr All-Wise.

'Oh yes,' answered he, 'I am Doctor All-Wise, sure enough.'

'Will you go with me, then,' said the nobleman, 'and get me back my money?'

'To be sure I will,' said the doctor; 'but my wife Grethel must go with me.'

The nobleman was pleased to hear this, made them both get into the carriage with him and away they all rode together. When they arrived at the nobleman's house dinner was already prepared, and he desired the doctor to sit down with him.

'My wife Grethel, too,' said the doctor.

As soon as the first servant brought in the first dish, which was some great delicacy, the doctor nudged his wife, and said – 'Grethel, that is the first,' meaning the first dish.

The servant overheard his remark, and thought he meant to say he was the first thief, which was actually the case, so he was sore troubled, and said to his comrades – 'The doctor knows everything. Things will certainly fall out ill, for he said I was the first thief.'

The second servant would not believe what he said, but at last he was obliged, for when he carried the second dish into the room, the doctor remarked to his wife – 'Grethel, that is the second.'

The second servant was now as much frightened as the first, and was pleased to leave the apartment. The third served no better, for the doctor said – 'Grethel, that is the third.'

Now the fourth carried in a dish which had a cover on it, and the nobleman desired the doctor to show his skill by guessing what was under the cover. Now it was a crab. The doctor looked at the dish, and then at the cover, and could not at all divine what they contained, nor how to get out of the scrape. At length, he said, half to himself and half aloud – 'Alas! Poor crab!'

When the nobleman heard this, he cried out – 'You have guessed it, and now I am sure you will know where my money is.'

The servant was greatly troubled at this, and he winked to the doctor to follow him out of the room, and no sooner did he do so than the whole four who had stolen the gold stood before him, and said that they would give it up instantly, and give him a good sum to boot, provided he would not betray them, for if he did their necks would pay for it. The doctor promised, and they conducted him to the place where the gold lay concealed. The doctor was well pleased to see it, and went back to the nobleman, and said – 'My lord, I will now search in my book and discover where the money is.'

Now the fifth servant had crept into an oven to hear what the doctor said. He sat for some time turning over the leaves of his A, B, C book, looking for the picture of the crowing cock, and as he did not find it readily, he exclaimed – 'I know you are in here, and you must come out.'

Then the man in the oven, thinking the doctor spoke of him, jumped out in a great fright, saying – 'The man knows everything.'

Then Doctor All-Wise showed the nobleman where the gold was hidden, but he said nothing as to who stole it. So he received a great reward from all parties and became a very famous man.

From: Folk-lore and Legends: Germany

The Boy Who Wanted More Cheese

Klaas Van Bommel was a Dutch boy, twelve years old, who lived where cows were plentiful. He was over five feet high, weighed a hundred pounds, and had rosy cheeks. His appetite was always good and his mother declared his stomach had no bottom. His hair was of a colour halfway between a carrot and a sweet potato. It was as thick as reeds in a swamp and was cut level, from under one ear to another.

Klaas stood in a pair of timber shoes, that made an awful rattle when he ran fast to catch a rabbit or scuffed slowly along to school over the brick road of his village. In summer Klaas was dressed in a rough, blue linen blouse. In winter he wore woollen breeches as wide as coffee bags. They were called bell trousers, and in shape were like a couple of cow-bells turned upwards. These were buttoned onto a thick warm jacket. Until he was five years old, Klaas was dressed like his sisters. Then, on his birthday, he had boy's clothes, with two pockets in them, of which he was proud enough.

Klaas was a farmer's boy. He had rye bread and fresh milk for breakfast. At dinner time, beside cheese and bread, he was given a plate heaped with boiled potatoes. Into these, he first plunged a fork and then dipped each round, white ball into a bowl of hot melted butter. Very quickly then did potato and butter disappear 'down the red lane.' At supper, he had bread and skim milk, left after the cream had been taken off, with a saucer, to make butter. Twice a week the children enjoyed a bowl of bonnyclabber or curds, with a little brown sugar sprinkled on the top. But at every meal, there was cheese, usually in thin slices, which the boy thought not thick enough. When Klaas went to bed he usually fell asleep as soon as his shock of yellow hair touched the pillow. In summertime he slept till the birds began to sing, at dawn. In winter, when the bed felt warm and Jack Frost was lively, he often heard the cows talking, in their way, before he jumped out of his bag of straw, which served for a mattress. The Van Bommels were not rich, but everything was shining clean.

There was always plenty to eat at the Van Bommels' house. Stacks of rye bread, a yard long and thicker than a man's arm, stood on end in the corner of the cool, stone-lined basement. The loaves of dough were put in the oven once a week. Baking time was a great event at the Van Bommels' and no men-folks were allowed in the kitchen on that day unless they were called in to help. As for the milk pails and pans, filled or emptied, scrubbed or set in the sun every day to dry, and the cheeses, piled up in the pantry, they seemed sometimes enough to feed a small army.

But Klaas always wanted more cheese. In other ways, he was a good boy, obedient at home, always ready to work on the cow farm, and diligent in school. But at the table, he never had enough. Sometimes his father laughed and asked him if he had a well, or a cave, under his jacket.

Klaas had three younger sisters, Trintjé, Annekė and Saartjé; which is Dutch for Kate, Annie and Sallie. These, their fond mother, who loved them dearly, called her 'orange blossoms'; but when at dinner, Klaas would keep on, dipping his potatoes into the hot butter, while others were all through, his mother would laugh and call him her Buttercup. But always Klaas wanted more cheese. When unusually greedy, she twitted him as a boy 'worse than Butter-and-Eggs'; that is, as troublesome as the yellow and white plant, called toad-flax, is to the farmer – very pretty, but nothing but a weed.

One summer's evening, after a good scolding, which he deserved well, Klaas moped and, almost crying, went to bed in bad humour. He had teased each one of his sisters to give him her bit of cheese, and this, added to his own slice, made his stomach feel as heavy as lead.

Klaas's bed was up in the garret. When the house was first built, one of the red tiles of the roof had been taken out and another one, made of glass, was put in its place. In the morning, this gave the boy light to put on his clothes. At night, in fair weather, it supplied air to his room.

A gentle breeze was blowing from the pine woods on the sandy slope, not far away. So Klaas climbed up on the stool to sniff the sweet piny doors. He thought he saw lights dancing under the tree. One beam seemed to approach his roof hole, and coming nearer played around the chimney. Then it passed to and fro in front of him. It seemed to whisper in his ear, as it moved by. It looked very much as if a hundred fireflies had united their cold light into one lamp. Then Klaas thought that the strange beams bore the shape of a lovely girl, but he only laughed at himself at the idea. Pretty soon, however, he thought the whisper became a voice. Again, he laughed so heartily, that he forgot his moping and the scolding his mother had given him. In fact, his eyes twinkled with delight, when the voice gave this invitation: 'There's plenty of cheese. Come with us.'

To make sure of it, the sleepy boy now rubbed his eyes and cocked his ears. Again, the light-bearer spoke to him: 'Come.'

Could it be? He had heard old people tell of the ladies of the wood, that whispered and warned travellers. In fact, he himself had often seen the 'fairies' ring' in the pine woods. To this, the flame-lady was inviting him.

Again and again, the moving, cold light circled around the red tile roof, which the moon, then rising and peeping over the chimneys, seemed to turn into silver plates. As the disc rose higher in the sky, he could hardly see the moving light, that had looked like a lady; but the voice, no longer a whisper, as at first, was now even plainer: 'There's plenty of cheese. Come with us.'

'I'll see what it is, anyhow,' said Klaas, as he drew on his thick woollen stockings and prepared to go downstairs and out, without waking a soul. At the door, he stepped into his wooden shoes. Just then the cat purred and rubbed up against his shins. He jumped, for he was scared; but looking down, for a moment, he saw the two balls of yellow fire in her head and knew what they were. Then he sped to the pine woods and towards the fairy ring.

What an odd sight! At first Klaas thought it was a circle of big fireflies. Then he saw clearly that there were dozens of pretty creatures, hardly as large as dolls, but as lively as crickets. They were as full of light, as if lamps had wings. Hand in hand, they flitted and danced around the ring of grass, as if this was fun.

Hardly had Klaas got over his first surprise, than of a sudden he felt himself surrounded by the fairies. Some of the strongest among them had left the main party in the circle and come to him. He felt himself pulled by their dainty fingers. One of them, the loveliest of all, whispered in his ear: 'Come, you must dance with us.'

Then a dozen of the pretty creatures murmured in chorus: 'Plenty of cheese here. Plenty of cheese here. Come, come!'

Upon this, the heels of Klaas seemed as light as a feather. In a moment, with both hands clasped in those of the fairies, he was dancing in high glee. It was as much fun as if he were at a festival, with a row of boys and girls, hand in hand, swinging along the streets, as Dutch maids and youth do, during festival week.

Klaas had not time to look hard at the fairies, for he was too full of the fun. He danced and danced, all night and until the sky in the east began to turn, first grey and then rosy. Then he tumbled down, tired out, and fell asleep. His head lay on the inner curve of the fairy ring, with his feet in the centre.

Klaas felt very happy, for he had no sense of being tired, and he did not know he was asleep. He thought his fairy partners, who had danced with him, were now waiting on him to bring him cheeses. With a golden knife, they sliced them off and fed him out of their own hands. How good it tasted! He thought now he could, and would, eat all the cheese he had longed for all his life. There was no mother to scold him, or daddy to shake his finger at him. How delightful!

But by and by, he wanted to stop eating and rest a while. His jaws were tired. His stomach seemed to be loaded with cannonballs. He gasped for breath.

But the fairies would not let him stop, for Dutch fairies never get tired. Flying out of the sky – from the north, south, east and west – they came, bringing cheeses. These they dropped down around him until the piles of the round masses threatened first to enclose him as with a wall, and then to overtop him. There were the red balls from Edam, the pink and yellow spheres from Gouda, and the grey loaf-shaped ones from Leyden. Down through the vista of sand, in the pine woods, he looked, and oh, horrors! There were the tallest and strongest of the fairies rolling along the huge, round, flat cheeses from Friesland! Any one of these was as big as a cartwheel, and would feed a regiment. The fairies trundled the heavy discs along as if they were playing with hoops. They shouted hilariously, as, with a pine stick, they beat them forward like boys at play. Farm cheese, factory cheese, Alkmaar cheese, and, to crown all, cheese from Limburg – which Klaas never could bear, because of its strong odour. Soon the cakes and balls were heaped so high around him that the boy, as he looked up, felt like a frog in a well. He groaned when he thought the high cheese walls were tottering to fall on him. Then he screamed, but the fairies thought he was making music. They, not being human, do not know how a boy feels.

At last, with a thick slice in one hand and a big hunk in the other, he could eat no more cheese; though the fairies, led by their queen, standing on one side, or hovering over his head, still urged him to take more.

At this moment, while afraid that he would burst, Klaas saw the pile of cheeses, as big as a house, topple over. The heavy mass fell inwards upon him. With a scream of terror, he thought himself crushed as flat as a Friesland cheese.

But he wasn't! Waking up and rubbing his eyes, he saw the red sun rising on the sand-dunes. Birds were singing and the cocks were crowing all around him, in chorus, as if saluting him. Just then also the village clock chimed out the hour. He felt his clothes. They were wet with dew. He sat up to look around. There were no fairies, but in his mouth was a bunch of grass which he had been chewing lustily.

Klaas never would tell the story of his night with the fairies, nor has he yet settled the question whether they left him because the cheese house of his dream had fallen, or because daylight had come.

From: Dutch Fairy Tales for Young Folks

The Three Sillies

ONCE UPON A time, there was a farmer and his wife who had one daughter, and she was courted by a gentleman. Every evening he used to come and see her, and stop to supper at the farmhouse, and the daughter used to be sent down into the cellar to draw the beer for supper. So one evening she had gone down to draw the beer, and she happened to look up at the ceiling while she was drawing, and she saw a mallet stuck in one of the beams. It must have been there a long, long time, but somehow or other she had never noticed it before, and she began a-thinking. And she thought it was very dangerous to have that mallet there, for she said to herself:

'Suppose him and me was to be married, and we was to have a son, and he was to grow up to be a man, and come down into the cellar to draw the beer, like as I'm doing now, and the mallet was to fall on his head and kill him, what a dreadful thing it would be!'

And she put down the candle and the jug and sat herself down and began a-crying.

Well, they began to wonder upstairs how it was that she was so long drawing the beer, and her mother went down to see after her, and she found her sitting on the settle crying, and the beer running over the floor.

'Why, whatever is the matter?' said her mother.

'Oh, mother!' says she, 'look at that horrid mallet! Suppose we was to be married, and was to have a son, and he was to grow up, and was to come down to the cellar to draw the beer, and the mallet was to fall on his head and kill him, what a dreadful thing it would be!'

'Dear, dear! what a dreadful thing it would be!' said the mother, and she sat her down aside of the daughter and started a-crying too. Then after a bit, the father began to wonder that they didn't come back, and he went down into the cellar to look after them himself, and there they two sat a-crying, and the beer running all over the floor.

'Whatever is the matter?' says he.

'Why,' says the mother, 'look at that horrid mallet. Just suppose, if our daughter and her sweetheart was to be married, and was to have a son, and he was to grow up, and was to come down into the cellar to draw the beer, and the mallet was to fall on his head and kill him, what a dreadful thing it would be!'

'Dear, dear, dear! So it would!' said the father, and he sat himself down aside of the other two, and started a-crying.

Now the gentleman got tired of stopping up in the kitchen by himself, and at last, he went down into the cellar too, to see what they were after; and there they three sat a-crying side by side, and the beer running all over the floor. And he ran straight and turned the tap. Then he said: 'Whatever are you three doing, sitting there crying, and letting the beer run all over the floor?'

'Oh!' says the father, 'look at that horrid mallet! Suppose you and our daughter was to be married, and was to have a son, and he was to grow up, and was to come down into the cellar to draw the beer, and the mallet was to fall on his head and kill him!'

And then they all started a-crying worse than before. But the gentleman burst out a-laughing, and reached up and pulled out the mallet, and then he said: 'I've travelled many miles, and I never met three such big sillies as you three before; and now I shall start out on my travels again, and when I can find three bigger sillies than you three, then I'll come back and marry your daughter.'

So he wished them goodbye, and started off on his travels, and left them all crying because the girl had lost her sweetheart.

Well, he set out, and he travelled a long way, and at last he came to a woman's cottage that had some grass growing on the roof. And the woman was trying to get her cow to go up a ladder to the grass, and the poor thing durst not go. So the gentleman asked the woman what she was doing.

'Why, look,' she said, 'look at all that beautiful grass. I'm going to get the cow onto the roof to eat it. She'll be quite safe, for I shall tie a string round her neck, and pass it down the chimney, and tie it to my wrist as I go about the house, so she can't fall off without my knowing it.'

'Oh, you poor silly!' said the gentleman, 'you should cut the grass and throw it down to the cow!'

But the woman thought it was easier to get the cow up the ladder than to get the grass down, so she pushed her and coaxed her and got her up, and tied a string round her neck, and passed it down the chimney, and fastened it to her own wrist. And the gentleman went on his way, but he hadn't gone far when the cow tumbled off the roof, and hung by the string tied around her neck, and it strangled her. And the weight of the cow tied to her wrist pulled the woman up the chimney, and she stuck fast halfway and was smothered in the soot.

Well, that was one big silly.

And the gentleman went on and on, and he went to an inn to stop the night, and they were so full at the inn that they had to put him in a double-bedded room, and another traveller was to sleep in the other bed. The other man was a very pleasant fellow, and they got very friendly together; but in the morning, when they were both getting up, the gentleman was surprised to see the other hang his trousers on the knobs of the chest of drawers and run across the room and try to jump into them, and he tried over and over again, and couldn't manage it; and the gentleman wondered whatever he was doing it for. At last, he stopped and wiped his face with his handkerchief.

'Oh dear,' he says, 'I do think trousers are the most awkward kind of clothes that ever were. I can't think who could have invented such things. It takes me the best part of an hour to get into mine every morning, and I get so hot! How do you manage yours?'

So the gentleman burst out a-laughing, and showed him how to put them on; and he was very much obliged to him, and said he never should have thought of doing it that way.

So that was another big silly.

Then the gentleman went on his travels again; and he came to a village, and outside the village there was a pond, and round the pond was a crowd of people. And they had got rakes, and brooms, and pitchforks, reaching into the pond; and the gentleman asked what was the matter.

'Why,' they say, 'matter enough! Moon's tumbled into the pond, and we can't rake her out anyhow!'

So the gentleman burst out a-laughing, and told them to look up into the sky, and that it was only the shadow in the water. But they wouldn't listen to him, and abused him shamefully, and he got away as quick as he could.

So there was a whole lot of sillies bigger than them three sillies at home. So the gentleman turned back home again and married the farmer's daughter, and if they didn't live happy for ever after, that's nothing to do with you or me.

From: English Fairy Tales

The Hare & the Lion

ONE DAY SOONGOO⌧RA, the hare, roaming through the forest in search of food, glanced up through the boughs of a very large calabash tree, and saw that a great hole in the upper part of the trunk was inhabited by bees; thereupon he returned to town in search of someone to go with him and help to get the honey.

As he was passing the house of Bookoo, the big rat, that worthy gentleman invited him in. So he went in, sat down, and remarked: 'My father has died, and has left me a hive of honey. I would like you to come and help me to eat it.'

Of course, Bookoo jumped at the offer, and he and the hare started off immediately.

When they arrived at the great calabash tree, Soongoora pointed out the bees' nest and said, 'Go on; climb up.'

So, taking some straw with them, they climbed up to the nest, lit the straw, smoked out the bees, put out the fire, and set to work eating the honey.

In the midst of the feast, who should appear at the foot of the tree but Sim⌧ba, the lion? Looking up, and seeing them eating, he asked, 'Who are you?'

Then Soongoora whispered to Bookoo, 'Hold your tongue; that old fellow is crazy.'

But in a very little while Simba roared out angrily: 'Who are you, I say? Speak, I tell you!'

This made Bookoo so scared that he blurted out, 'It's only us!'

Upon this the hare said to him: 'You just wrap me up in this straw, call to the lion to keep out of the way, and then throw me down. Then you'll see what will happen.'

So Bookoo, the big rat, wrapped Soongoora, the hare, in the straw, and then called to Simba, the lion, 'Stand back; I'm going to throw this straw down, and then I'll come down myself.'

When Simba stepped back out of the way, Bookoo threw down the straw, and as it lay on the ground Soongoora crept out and ran away while the lion was looking up.

After waiting a minute or two, Simba roared out, 'Well, come down, I say!' and, there being no help for it, the big rat came down.

As soon as he was within reach, the lion caught hold of him, and asked, 'Who was up there with you?'

'Why,' said Bookoo, 'Soongoora, the hare. Didn't you see him when I threw him down?'

'Of course I didn't see him,' replied the lion, in an incredulous tone, and, without wasting further time, he ate the big rat, and then searched around for the hare, but could not find him.

Three days later, Soongoora called on his acquaintance, Kobay, the tortoise, and said to him, 'Let us go and eat some honey.'

'Whose honey?' inquired Kobay, cautiously.

'My father's,' Soongoora replied.

'Oh, all right; I'm with you,' said the tortoise, eagerly; and away they went.

When they arrived at the great calabash tree they climbed up with their straw, smoked out the bees, sat down, and began to eat.

Just then Mr. Simba, who owned the honey, came out again, and, looking up, inquired, 'Who are you, up there?'

Soongoora whispered to Kobay, 'Keep quiet;' but when the lion repeated his question angrily, Kobay became suspicious, and said: 'I will speak. You told me this honey was yours; am I right in suspecting that it belongs to Simba?'

So, when the lion asked again, 'Who are you?' he answered, 'It's only us.'

The lion said, 'Come down, then;' and the tortoise answered, 'We're coming.'

Now, Simba had been keeping an eye open for Soongoora since the day he caught Bookoo, the big rat, and, suspecting that he was up there with Kobay, he said to himself, 'I've got him this time, sure.'

Seeing that they were caught again, Soongoora said to the tortoise: 'Wrap me up in the straw, tell Simba to stand out of the way, and then throw me down. I'll wait for you below. He can't hurt you, you know.'

'All right,' said Kobay; but while he was wrapping the hare up he said to himself: 'This fellow wants to run away, and leave me to bear the lion's anger. He shall get caught first.'

Therefore, when he had bundled him up, he called out, 'Soongoora is coming!' and threw him down.

So Simba caught the hare, and, holding him with his paw, said, 'Now, what shall I do with you?'

The hare replied, 'It's of no use for you to try to eat me; I'm awfully tough.'

'What would be the best thing to do with you, then?' asked Simba.

'I think,' said Soongoora, 'you should take me by the tail, whirl me around, and knock me against the ground. Then you may be able to eat me.'

So the lion, being deceived, took him by the tail and whirled him around, but just as he was going to knock him on the ground he slipped out of his grasp and ran away, and Simba had the mortification of losing him again.

Angry and disappointed, he turned to the tree and called to Kobay, 'You come down, too.'

When the tortoise reached the ground, the lion said, 'You're pretty hard; what can I do to make you eatable?'

'Oh, that's easy,' laughed Kobay; 'just put me in the mud and rub my back with your paw until my shell comes off.'

Immediately on hearing this, Simba carried Kobay to the water, placed him in the mud, and began, as he supposed, to rub his back; but the tortoise had slipped away, and the lion continued rubbing on a piece of rock until his paws were raw. When he glanced down at them he saw they were bleeding, and, realizing that he had again been outwitted, he said, 'Well, the hare has done me today, but I'll go hunting now until I find him.'

So Simba, the lion, set out immediately in search of Soongoora, the hare, and as he went along he inquired of every one he met, 'Where is the house of Soongoora?'

But each person he asked answered, 'I do not know.'

For the hare had said to his wife, 'Let us remove from this house.'

Therefore, the folks in that neighbourhood had no knowledge of his whereabouts. Simba, however, went along, continuing his inquiries, until presently one answered, 'That is his house on the top of the mountain.'

Without loss of time the lion climbed the mountain, and soon arrived at the place indicated, only to find that there was no one at home. This, however, did not trouble him; on the contrary, saying to himself, 'I'll hide myself inside, and when Soongoora and his wife come home I'll eat them both,' he entered the house and lay down, awaiting their arrival.

Pretty soon along came the hare with his wife, not thinking of any danger; but he very soon discovered the marks of the lion's paws on the steep path. Stopping at once, he said to Mrs. Soongoora: 'You go back, my dear. Simba, the lion, has passed this way, and I think he must be looking for me.'

But she replied, 'I will not go back; I will follow you, my husband.'

Although greatly pleased at this proof of his wife's affection, Soongoora said firmly: 'No, no; you have friends to go to. Go back.'

So he persuaded her, and she went back; but he kept on, following the footmarks, and saw – as he had suspected – that they went into his house.

'Ah!' said he to himself, 'Mr. Lion is inside, is he?'

Then, cautiously going back a little way, he called out: 'How d'ye do, house? How d'ye do?'

Waiting a moment, he remarked loudly: 'Well, this is very strange! Every day, as I pass this place, I say, "How d'ye do, house?" and the house always answers, "How d'ye do?" There must be someone inside to-day.'

When the lion heard this he called out, 'How d'ye do?'

Then Soongoora burst out laughing, and shouted: 'Oho, Mr. Simba! You're inside, and I'll bet you want to eat me; but first tell me where you ever heard of a house talking!'

Upon this the lion, seeing how he had been fooled, replied angrily, 'You wait until I get hold of you; that's all.'

'Oh, I think you'll have to do the waiting,' cried the hare; and then he ran away, the lion following.

But it was of no use. Soongoora completely tired out old Simba, who, saying, 'That rascal has beaten me; I don't want to have anything more to do with him,' returned to his home under the great calabash tree.

From: Zanzibar Tales

The Yellow Dwarf

ONCE UPON A time, there lived a queen who had been the mother of a great many children, and of them all only one daughter was left. But then SHE was worth at least a thousand.

Her mother, who, since the death of the King, her father, had nothing in the world she cared for so much as this little Princess, was so terribly afraid of losing her that she quite spoiled her, and never tried to correct any of her faults. The consequence was that this little person, who was as pretty as possible, and was one day to wear a crown, grew up so proud and so much in love with her own beauty that she despised everyone else in the world.

The Queen, her mother, by her caresses and flatteries, helped to make her believe that there was nothing too good for her. She was dressed almost always in the prettiest frocks, as a fairy, or as a queen going out to hunt, and the ladies of the Court followed her dressed as forest fairies.

And to make her more vain than ever the Queen caused her portrait to be taken by the cleverest painters and sent it to several neighbouring kings with whom she was very friendly.

When they saw this portrait they fell in love with the Princess – every one of them, but upon each, it had a different effect. One fell ill, one went quite crazy, and a few of the luckiest set off to see her as soon as possible, but these poor princes became her slaves the moment they set eyes on her.

Never has there been a gayer Court. Twenty delightful kings did everything they could think of to make themselves agreeable, and after having spent ever so much money in giving a single entertainment thought themselves very lucky if the Princess said 'That's pretty.'

All this admiration vastly pleased the Queen. Not a day passed but she received seven or eight thousand sonnets, and as many elegies, madrigals, and songs, which were sent her by all the poets in the world. All the prose and the poetry that was written just then was about Bellissima – for that was the Princess's name – and all the bonfires that they had were made of these verses, which crackled and sparkled better than any other sort of wood.

Bellissima was already fifteen years old, and every one of the Princes wished to marry her, but not one dared to say so. How could they when they knew that any of them might have cut off his head five or six times a day just to please her, and she would have thought it a mere trifle, so little did she care? You may imagine how hard-hearted her lovers thought her; and the Queen, who wished to see her married, did not know how to persuade her to think of it seriously.

'Bellissima,' she said, 'I do wish you would not be so proud. What makes you despise all these nice kings? I wish you to marry one of them, and you do not try to please me.'

'I am so happy,' Bellissima answered, 'do leave me in peace, madam. I don't want to care for anyone.'

'But you would be very happy with any of these Princes,' said the Queen, 'and I shall be very angry if you fall in love with anyone who is not worthy of you.'

But the Princess thought so much of herself that she did not consider any one of her lovers clever or handsome enough for her; and her mother, who was getting really angry at her determination not to be married, began to wish that she had not allowed her to have her own way so much.

At last, not knowing what else to do, she resolved to consult a certain witch who was called 'The Fairy of the Desert.' Now this was very difficult to do, as she was guarded by some terrible lions; but happily the Queen had heard a long time before that whoever wanted to pass these lions safely must throw to them a cake made of millet flour, sugar candy, and crocodile's eggs. This cake she prepared with her own hands, and putting it in a little basket, she set out to seek the Fairy. But as she was not used to walking far, she soon felt very tired and sat down at the foot of a tree to rest, and presently fell fast asleep. When she awoke she was dismayed to find her basket empty. The cake was all gone! And, to make matters worse, at that moment she heard the roaring of the great lions, who had found out that she was near and were coming to look for her.

'What shall I do?' she cried; 'I shall be eaten up,' and being too frightened to run a single step, she began to cry, and leaned against the tree under which she had been asleep.

Just then she heard someone say: 'H'm, h'm!'

She looked all around her, and then up the tree, and there she saw a little tiny man, who was eating oranges.

'Oh! Queen,' said he, 'I know you very well, and I know how much afraid you are of the lions; and you are quite right too, for they have eaten many other people: and what can you expect, as you have not any cake to give them?'

'I must make up my mind to die,' said the poor Queen. 'Alas! I should not care so much if only my dear daughter were married.'

'Oh! You have a daughter,' cried the Yellow Dwarf (who was so called because he WAS a dwarf and had such a yellow face, and lived in the orange tree). 'I'm really glad to hear that, for I've been looking for a wife all over the world. Now, if you will promise that she shall marry me, not one of the lions, tigers, or bears shall touch you.'

The Queen looked at him and was almost as much afraid of his ugly little face as she had been of the lions before, so that she could not speak a word.

'What! You hesitate, madam,' cried the Dwarf. 'You must be very fond of being eaten up alive.'

And, as he spoke, the Queen saw the lions, which were running down a hill toward them.

Each one had two heads, eight feet, and four rows of teeth, and their skins were as hard as turtle shells, and were bright red.

At this dreadful sight, the poor Queen, who was trembling like a dove when it sees a hawk, cried out as loud as she could, 'Oh! dear Mr. Dwarf, Bellissima shall marry you.'

'Oh, indeed!' said he disdainfully. 'Bellissima is pretty enough, but I don't particularly want to marry her – you can keep her.'

'Oh! noble sir,' said the Queen in great distress, 'do not refuse her. She is the most charming Princess in the world.'

'Oh! well,' he replied, 'out of charity I will take her; but be sure and don't forget that she is mine.'

As he spoke a little door opened in the trunk of the orange tree, in rushed the Queen, only just in time, and the door shut with a bang in the faces of the lions.

The Queen was so confused that at first, she did not notice another little door in the orange tree, but presently it opened and she found herself in a field of thistles and nettles. It was encircled by a muddy ditch, and a little further on was a tiny thatched cottage, out of which came the Yellow Dwarf with a very jaunty air. He wore wooden shoes and a little yellow coat, and as he had no hair and very long ears he looked altogether a shocking little object.

'I am delighted,' said he to the Queen, 'that, as you are to be my mother-in-law, you should see the little house in which your Bellissima will live with me. With these thistles and nettles, she can feed a donkey which she can ride whenever she likes; under this humble roof no weather can hurt her; she will drink the water of this brook and eat frogs – which grow very fat about here; and then she will have me always with her, handsome, agreeable, and gay as you see me now. For if her shadow stays by her more closely than I do I shall be surprised.'

The unhappy Queen. seeing all at once what a miserable life her daughter would have with this Dwarf could not bear the idea, and fell down insensible without saying a word.

When she revived she found to her great surprise that she was lying in her own bed at home, and, what was more, that she had on the loveliest lace nightcap that she had ever seen in her life. At first, she thought that all her adventures, the terrible lions, and her promise to the Yellow Dwarf that he should marry Bellissima, must have been a dream, but there was the new cap with its beautiful ribbon and lace to remind her that it was all true, which made her so unhappy that she could neither eat, drink, nor sleep for thinking of it.

The Princess, who, in spite of her wilfulness, really loved her mother with all her heart, was much grieved when she saw her looking so sad, and often asked her what was the matter; but the Queen, who didn't want her to find out the truth, only said that she was ill, or that one of her neighbours was threatening to make war against her. Bellissima knew quite well that something was being hidden from her – and that neither of these was the real reason of the Queen's uneasiness. So she made up her mind that she would go and consult the Fairy of the Desert about it, especially as she had often heard how wise she was, and she thought that at the same time, she might ask her advice as to whether it would be as well to be married, or not.

So, with great care, she made some of the proper cake to pacify the lions, and one night went up to her room very early, pretending that she was going to bed; but instead of that, she wrapped herself in a long white veil, and went down a secret staircase, and set off all by herself to find the Witch.

But when she got as far as the same fatal orange tree, and saw it covered with flowers and fruit, she stopped and began to gather some of the oranges – and then, putting down her basket, she sat down to eat them. But when it was time to go on again the basket had disappeared and, though she looked everywhere, not a trace of it could she find. The more she hunted for it, the more frightened she got, and at last she began to cry. Then all at once she saw before her the Yellow Dwarf.

'What's the matter with you, my pretty one?' said he. 'What are you crying about?'

'Alas!' she answered; 'no wonder that I am crying, seeing that I have lost the basket of cake that was to help me to get safely to the cave of the Fairy of the Desert.'

'And what do you want with her, pretty one?' said the little monster, 'for I am a friend of hers, and, for the matter of that, I am quite as clever as she is.'

'The Queen, my mother,' replied the Princess, 'has lately fallen into such deep sadness that I fear that she will die; and I am afraid that perhaps I am the cause of it, for she very much wishes me to be married, and I must tell you truly that as yet I have not found anyone I consider worthy to be my husband. So for all these reasons I wished to talk to the Fairy.'

'Do not give yourself any further trouble, Princess,' answered the Dwarf. 'I can tell you all you want to know better than she could. The Queen, your mother, has promised you in marriage.'

'Has promised ME!' interrupted the Princess. 'Oh! no. I'm sure she has not. She would have told me if she had. I am too much interested in the matter for her to promise anything without my consent – you must be mistaken.'

'Beautiful Princess,' cried the Dwarf suddenly, throwing himself on his knees before her, 'I flatter myself that you will not be displeased at her choice when I tell you that it is to ME she has promised the happiness of marrying you.'

'You!' cried Bellissima, starting back. 'My mother wishes me to marry you! How can you be so silly as to think of such a thing?'

'Oh! It isn't that I care much to have that honour,' cried the Dwarf angrily; 'but here are the lions coming; they'll eat you up in three mouthfuls, and there will be an end of you and your pride.'

And, indeed, at that moment the poor Princess heard their dreadful howls coming nearer and nearer. 'What shall I do?' she cried. 'Must all my happy days come to an end like this?'

The malicious Dwarf looked at her and began to laugh spitefully. 'At least,' said he, 'you have the satisfaction of dying unmarried. A lovely Princess like you must surely prefer to die rather than be the wife of a poor little dwarf like myself.'

'Oh, don't be angry with me,' cried the Princess, clasping her hands. 'I'd rather marry all the dwarfs in the world than die in this horrible way.'

'Look at me well, Princess, before you give me your word,' said he. 'I don't want you to promise me in a hurry.'

'Oh!' cried she, 'the lions are coming. I have looked at you enough. I am so frightened. Save me this minute, or I shall die of terror.'

Indeed, as she spoke she fell down insensible, and when she recovered she found herself in her own little bed at home; how she got there she could not tell, but she was dressed in the most beautiful lace and ribbons, and on her finger was a little ring, made of a single red hair, which fitted so tightly that, try as she might, she could not get it off.

When the Princess saw all these things, and remembered what had happened, she, too, fell into the deepest sadness, which surprised and alarmed the whole Court, and the Queen more than anyone else. A hundred times she asked Bellissima if anything was the matter with her; but she always said that there was nothing

At last the chief men of the kingdom, anxious to see their Princess married, sent to the Queen to beg her to choose a husband for her as soon as possible. She replied that nothing would please her better, but that her daughter seemed so unwilling to marry, and she recommended them to go and talk to the Princess about it themselves so this they at once did. Now Bellissima was much less proud since her adventure with the Yellow Dwarf, and she could not think of a better way of getting rid of the little monster than to marry some powerful king, therefore she replied to their request much more favourably than they had hoped, saying that, though she was very happy as she was, still, to please them, she would consent to marry the King of the Gold Mines. Now he was a very handsome and powerful Prince, who had been in love with the Princess for years, but had not thought that she would ever care about him at all. You can easily imagine how delighted he was when he heard the news, and how angry it made all the other kings to lose forever the hope of marrying the Princess; but, after all, Bellissima could not have married twenty kings – indeed, she had found it quite difficult enough to choose one, for her vanity made her believe that there was nobody in the world who was worthy of her.

Preparations were begun at once for the grandest wedding that had ever been held at the palace. The King of the Gold Mines sent such immense sums of money that the whole sea was covered with the ships that brought it. Messengers were sent to all the gayest and most refined Courts, particularly to the Court of France, to seek out everything rare and precious to adorn the Princess, although her beauty was so perfect that nothing she wore could make her look prettier. At least that is what the King of the Gold Mines thought, and he was never happy unless he was with her.

As for the Princess, the more she saw of the King the more she liked him; he was so generous, so handsome and clever, that at last she was almost as much in love with him as he was with her. How happy they were as they wandered about in the beautiful gardens together, sometimes listening to sweet music! And the King used to write songs for Bellissima. This is one that she liked very much:

In the forest, all is gay
When my Princess walks that way.
All the blossoms then are found
Downward fluttering to the ground,

hoping she may tread on them.
And bright flowers on slender stem
Gaze up at her as she passes
Brushing lightly through the grasses.
Oh! My Princess, birds above
Echo back our songs of love,
as through this enchanted land
Blithe we wander, hand in hand.

They really were as happy as the day was long. All the King's unsuccessful rivals had gone home in despair. They said goodbye to the Princess so sadly that she could not help being sorry for them.

'Ah! Madam,' the King of the Gold Mines said to her 'how is this? Why do you waste your pity on these princes, who love you so much that all their trouble would be well repaid by a single smile from you?'

'I should be sorry,' answered Bellissima, 'if you had not noticed how much I pitied these princes who were leaving me forever; but for you, sire, it is very different: you have every reason to be pleased with me, but they are going sorrowfully away, so you must not grudge them my compassion.'

The King of the Gold Mines was quite overcome by the Princess's good-natured way of taking his interference, and, throwing himself at her feet, he kissed her hand a thousand times and begged her to forgive him.

At last the happy day came. Everything was ready for Bellissima's wedding. The trumpets sounded, all the streets of the town were hung with flags and strewn with flowers, and the people ran in crowds to the great square before the palace. The Queen was so overjoyed that she had hardly been able to sleep at all, and she got up before it was light to give the necessary orders and to choose the jewels that the Princess was to wear. These were nothing less than diamonds, even to her shoes, which were covered with them, and her dress of silver brocade was embroidered with a dozen of the sun's rays. You may imagine how much these had cost; but then nothing could have been more brilliant, except the beauty of the Princess! Upon her head, she wore a splendid crown, her lovely hair waved nearly to her feet, and her stately figure could easily be distinguished among all the ladies who attended her.

The King of the Gold Mines was not less noble and splendid; it was easy to see by his face how happy he was, and everyone who went near him returned loaded with presents, for all around the great banqueting hall had been arranged a thousand barrels full of gold, and numberless bags made of velvet embroidered with pearls and filled with money, each one containing at least a hundred thousand gold pieces, which were given away to everyone who liked to hold out his hand, which numbers of people hastened to do, you may be sure – indeed, some found this by far the most amusing part of the wedding festivities.

The Queen and the Princess were just ready to set out with the King when they saw, advancing toward them from the end of the long gallery, two great basilisks, dragging after them a very badly made box; behind them came a tall old woman, whose ugliness was even more surprising than her extreme old age. She wore a ruff of black taffeta, a red velvet hood, and a farthingale all in rags, and she leaned heavily upon a crutch. This strange old woman, without saying a single word, hobbled three times around the gallery, followed by the basilisks, then stopping in the middle, and brandishing her crutch threateningly, she cried:

'Ho, ho, Queen! Ho, ho, Princess! Do you think you are going to break with impunity the promise that you made to my friend the Yellow Dwarf? I am the Fairy of the Desert; without the Yellow Dwarf and his orange tree my great lions would soon have eaten you up, I can tell you, and in Fairyland we do not suffer ourselves to be insulted like this. Make up your minds at once what you will do, for I vow that you shall marry the Yellow Dwarf. If you don't, may I burn my crutch!'

'Ah! Princess,' said the Queen, weeping, 'what is this that I hear? What have you promised?'

'Ah! My mother,' replied Bellissima sadly, 'what did YOU promise, yourself?'

The King of the Gold Mines, indignant at being kept from his happiness by this wicked old woman, went up to her, and threatening her with his sword, said: 'Get away out of my country at once, and forever, miserable creature, lest I take your life, and so rid myself of your malice.'

He had hardly spoken these words when the lid of the box fell back on the floor with a terrible noise, and to their horror out sprang the Yellow Dwarf, mounted upon a great Spanish cat. 'Rash youth!' he cried, rushing between the Fairy of the Desert and the King. 'Dare to lay a finger upon this illustrious Fairy! Your quarrel is with me only. I am your enemy and your rival. That faithless Princess who would have married you is promised to me. See if she has not upon her finger a ring made of one of my hairs. Just try to take it off, and you will soon find out that I am more powerful than you are!'

'Wretched little monster!' said the King; 'do you dare to call yourself the Princess's lover, and to lay claim to such a treasure? Do you know that you are a dwarf – that you are so ugly that one cannot bear to look at you – and that I should have killed you myself long before this if you had been worthy of such a glorious death?'

The Yellow Dwarf, deeply enraged at these words, set spurs to his cat, which yelled horribly, and leapt hither and thither – terrifying everybody except the brave King, who pursued the Dwarf closely, till he, drawing a great knife with which he was armed, challenged the King to meet him in single combat, and rushed down into the courtyard of the palace with a terrible clatter. The King, quite provoked, followed him hastily, but they had hardly taken their places facing one another, and the whole Court had only just had time to rush out upon the balconies to watch what was going on, when suddenly the sun became as red as blood, and it was so dark that they could scarcely see at all. The thunder crashed, and the lightning seemed as if it must burn up everything; the two basilisks appeared, one on each side of the bad Dwarf, like giants, mountains high, and fire flew from their mouths and ears, until they looked like flaming furnaces. None of these things could terrify the noble young King, and the boldness of his looks and actions reassured those who were looking on, and perhaps even embarrassed the Yellow Dwarf himself; but even HIS courage gave way when he saw what was happening to his beloved Princess. For the Fairy of the Desert, looking more terrible than before, mounted upon a winged griffin, and with long snakes coiled round her neck, had given her such a blow with the lance she carried that Bellissima fell into the Queen's arms bleeding and senseless. Her fond mother, feeling as much hurt by the blow as the Princess herself, uttered such piercing cries and lamentations that the King, hearing them, entirely lost his courage and presence of mind. Giving up the combat, he flew toward the Princess, to rescue or to die with her; but the Yellow Dwarf was too quick for him. Leaping with his Spanish cat upon the balcony, he snatched Bellissima from the Queen's arms, and before any of the ladies of the Court could stop him he had sprung upon the roof of the palace and disappeared with his prize.

The King, motionless with horror, looked on despairingly at this dreadful occurrence, which he was quite powerless to prevent, and to make matters worse his sight failed him, everything became dark, and he felt himself carried along through the air by a strong hand.

This new misfortune was the work of the wicked Fairy of the Desert, who had come with the Yellow Dwarf to help him carry off the Princess, and had fallen in love with the handsome young King of the Gold Mines directly she saw him. She thought that if she carried him off to some frightful cavern and chained him to a rock, then the fear of death would make him forget Bellissima and become her slave. So, as soon as they reached the place, she gave him back his sight, but without releasing him from his chains, and by her magic power she appeared before him as a young and beautiful fairy, and pretended to have come there quite by chance.

'What do I see? she cried. 'Is it YOU, dear Prince? What misfortune has brought you to this dismal place?'

The King, who was quite deceived by her altered appearance, replied: 'Alas! beautiful Fairy, the fairy who brought me here first took away my sight, but by her voice, I recognized her as the Fairy of the Desert, though what she should have carried me off for I cannot tell you.'

'Ah!' cried the pretended Fairy, 'if you have fallen into HER hands, you won't get away until you have married her. She has carried off more than one Prince like this, and she will certainly have anything she takes a fancy to.'

While she was thus pretending to be sorry for the King, he suddenly noticed her feet, which were like those of a gryphon, and knew in a moment that this must be the Fairy of the Desert, for her feet were the one thing she could not change, however pretty she might make her face.

Without seeming to have noticed anything, he said, in a confidential way: 'Not that I have any dislike to the Fairy of the Desert, but I really cannot endure the way in which she protects the Yellow Dwarf and keeps me chained here like a criminal. It is true that I love a charming princess, but if the Fairy should set me free my gratitude would oblige me to love her only.'

'Do you really mean what you say, Prince?' said the Fairy, quite deceived.

'Surely,' replied the Prince; 'how could I deceive you? You see it is so much more flattering to my vanity to be loved by a fairy than by a simple princess. But, even if I am dying of love for her, I shall pretend to hate her until I am set free.'

The Fairy of the Desert, quite taken in by these words, resolved at once to transport the Prince to a pleasanter place. So, making him mount her chariot, to which she had harnessed swans instead of the bats which generally drew it, away she flew with him. But imagine the distress of the Prince when, from the giddy height at which they were rushing through the air, he saw his beloved Princess in a castle built of polished steel, the walls of which reflected the sun's rays so hotly that no one could approach it without being burnt to a cinder! Bellissima was sitting in a little thicket by a brook, leaning her head upon her hand and weeping bitterly, but just as they passed she looked up and saw the King and the Fairy of the Desert. Now, the Fairy was so clever that she could not only seem beautiful to the King, but even the poor Princess thought her the most lovely being she had ever seen.

'What!' she cried; 'was I not unhappy enough in this lonely castle to which that frightful Yellow Dwarf brought me? Must I also be made to know that the King of the Gold Mines ceased to love me as soon as he lost sight of me? But who can my rival be, whose fatal beauty is greater than mine?'

While she was saying this, the King, who really loved her as much as ever, was feeling terribly sad at being so rapidly torn away from his beloved Princess, but he knew too well how powerful the Fairy was to have any hope of escaping from her except by great patience and cunning.

The Fairy of the Desert had also seen Bellissima, and she tried to read in the King's eyes the effect that this unexpected sight had had upon him.

'No one can tell you what you wish to know better than I can,' said he. 'This chance meeting with an unhappy princess for whom I once had a passing fancy, before I was lucky enough to meet you, has affected me a little, I admit, but you are so much more to me than she is that I would rather die than leave you.'

'Ah, Prince,' she said, 'can I believe that you really love me so much?'

'Time will show, madam,' replied the King; 'but if you wish to convince me that you have some regard for me, do not, I beg of you, refuse to aid Bellissima.'

'Do you know what you are asking?' said the Fairy of the Desert, frowning, and looking at him suspiciously. 'Do you want me to employ my art against the Yellow Dwarf, who is my best friend, and take away from him a proud princess whom I can but look upon as my rival?'

The King sighed, but made no answer – indeed, what was there to be said to such a clear-sighted person? At last, they reached a vast meadow, gay with all sorts of flowers; a deep river surrounded it, and many little brooks murmured softly under the shady trees, where it was always cool and fresh. A little way off stood a splendid palace, the walls of which were of transparent emeralds. As soon as the swans which drew the Fairy's chariot had alighted under a porch, which was paved with diamonds and had arches of rubies, they were greeted on all sides by thousands of beautiful beings, who came to meet them joyfully, singing these words:

'When Love within a heart would reign,
Useless to strive against him 'tis.
The proud but feel a sharper pain,
and make a greater triumph his.'

The Fairy of the Desert was delighted to hear them sing of her triumphs; she led the King into the most splendid room that can be imagined, and left him alone for a little while, just that he might not feel that he was a prisoner; but he felt sure that she had not really gone quite away, but was watching him from some hiding place. So walking up to a great mirror, he said to it, 'Trusty counsellor, let me see what I can do to make myself agreeable to the charming Fairy of the Desert; for I can think of nothing but how to please her.'

And he at once set to work to curl his hair, and, seeing upon a table a grander coat than his own, he put it on carefully. The Fairy came back so delighted that she could not conceal her joy.

'I am quite aware of the trouble you have taken to please me,' said she, 'and I must tell you that you have succeeded perfectly already. You see it is not difficult to do if you really care for me.'

The King, who had his own reasons for wishing to keep the old Fairy in a good humour, did not spare pretty speeches, and after a time he was allowed to walk by himself upon the seashore. The Fairy of the Desert had by her enchantments raised such a terrible storm that the boldest pilot would not venture out in it, so she was not afraid of her prisoner's being able to escape, and he found it some relief to think sadly over his terrible situation without being interrupted by his cruel captor.

Presently, after walking wildly up and down, he wrote these verses upon the sand with his stick:

'At last may I upon this shore
Lighten my sorrow with soft tears.
Alas! Alas! I see no more
My Love, who yet my sadness cheers.
And thou, O raging, stormy Sea,
stirred by wild winds, from depth to height,
thou hold'st my loved one far from me,
And I am captive to thy might.
My heart is still more wild than thine,
For Fate is cruel unto me.
Why must I thus in exile pine?
Why is my Princess snatched from me?
O! lovely Nymphs, from ocean caves,
who know how sweet true love may be,
come up and calm the furious waves
and set a desperate lover free!'

While he was still writing he heard a voice which attracted his attention in spite of himself. Seeing that the waves were rolling in higher than ever, he looked all around, and presently saw a lovely lady floating gently toward him upon the crest of a huge billow, her long hair spread all about her; in one hand she held a mirror, and in the other a comb, and instead of feet she had a beautiful tail like a fish, with which she swam.

The King was struck dumb with astonishment at this unexpected sight; but as soon as she came within speaking distance, she said to him, 'I know how sad you are at losing your Princess and being kept a prisoner by the Fairy of the Desert; if you like I will help you to escape from this fatal place, where you may otherwise have to drag on a weary existence for thirty years or more.'

The King of the Gold Mines hardly knew what answer to make to this proposal. Not because he did not wish very much to escape, but he was afraid that this might be only another device by which the Fairy of the Desert was trying to deceive him. As he hesitated the Mermaid, who guessed his thoughts, said to him: 'You may trust me: I am not trying to entrap you. I am so angry with the Yellow Dwarf and the Fairy of the Desert that I am not likely to wish to help them, especially since I constantly see your poor Princess, whose beauty and goodness make me pity her so much; and I tell you that if you will have confidence in me I will help you to escape.'

'I trust you absolutely,' cried the King, 'and I will do whatever you tell me; but if you have seen my Princess I beg of you to tell me how she is and what is happening to her.'

'We must not waste time in talking,' said she. 'Come with me and I will carry you to the Castle of Steel, and we will leave upon this shore a figure so like you that even the Fairy herself will be deceived by it.'

So saying, she quickly collected a bundle of sea-weed, and, blowing it three times, she said:

'My friendly seaweeds, I order you to stay here stretched upon the sand until the Fairy of the Desert comes to take you away.'

And at once the sea-weeds became like the King, who stood looking at them in great astonishment, for they were even dressed in a coat like his, but they lay there pale and still as the King himself might have lain if one of the great waves had overtaken him and thrown him senseless upon the shore. And then the Mermaid caught up the King, and away they swam joyfully together.

'Now,' said she, 'I have time to tell you about the Princess. In spite of the blow which the Fairy of the Desert gave her, the Yellow Dwarf compelled her to mount behind him upon his terrible Spanish cat; but she soon fainted away with pain and terror, and did not recover till they were within the walls of his frightful Castle of Steel. Here she was received by the prettiest girls it was possible to find, who had been carried there by the Yellow Dwarf, who hastened to wait upon her and showed her every possible attention. She was laid upon a couch covered with cloth of gold, embroidered with pearls as big as nuts.'

'Ah!' interrupted the King of the Gold Mines, 'if Bellissima forgets me, and consents to marry him, I shall break my heart.'

'You need not be afraid of that,' answered the Mermaid, 'the Princess thinks of no one but you, and the frightful Dwarf cannot persuade her to look at him.'

'Pray go on with your story,' said the King.

'What more is there to tell you?' replied the Mermaid. 'Bellissima was sitting in the wood when you passed, and saw you with the Fairy of the Desert, who was so cleverly disguised that the Princess took her to be prettier than herself; you may imagine her despair, for she thought that you had fallen in love with her.'

'She believes that I love her!' cried the King. 'What a fatal mistake! What is to be done to undeceive her?'

'You know best,' answered the Mermaid, smiling kindly at him. 'When people are as much in love with one another as you two are, they don't need advice from anyone else.'

As she spoke they reached the Castle of Steel, the side next the sea being the only one which the Yellow Dwarf had left unprotected by the dreadful burning walls.

'I know quite well,' said the Mermaid, 'that the Princess is sitting by the brook-side, just where you saw her as you passed, but as you will have many enemies to fight with before you can reach her, take this sword; armed with it you may dare any danger, and overcome the greatest difficulties, only beware of one thing – that is, never to let it fall from your hand. Farewell; now I will wait by that rock, and if you need my help in carrying off your beloved Princess I will not fail you, for the Queen, her mother, is my best friend, and it was for her sake that I went to rescue you.'

So saying, she gave to the King a sword made from a single diamond, which was more brilliant than the sun. He could not find words to express his gratitude, but he begged her to believe that he fully appreciated the importance of her gift, and would never forget her help and kindness.

We must now go back to the Fairy of the Desert. When she found that the King did not return, she hastened out to look for him, and reached the shore, with a hundred of the ladies of her train, loaded with splendid presents for him. Some carried baskets full of diamonds, others golden cups of wonderful workmanship, and amber, coral, and pearls, others, again, balanced upon their heads bales of the richest and most beautiful stuffs, while the rest brought fruit and flowers, and even birds. But what was the horror of the Fairy, who followed this gay troop, when she saw, stretched upon the sands, the image of the King which the Mermaid had made with the seaweeds. Struck with astonishment and sorrow, she uttered a terrible cry, and threw herself down beside the pretended King, weeping, and howling, and calling upon her eleven sisters, who were also fairies, and who came to her assistance. But they were all taken in by the image of the King, for, clever as they were, the Mermaid was still cleverer, and all they could do was to help the Fairy of the Desert to make a wonderful monument over what they thought was the grave of the King of the Gold Mines. But while they were collecting jasper and porphyry, agate and marble, gold and bronze, statues and devices, to immortalize the King's memory, he was thanking the good Mermaid and begging her still to help him, which she graciously promised to do as she disappeared; and then he set out for the Castle of Steel.

He walked fast, looking anxiously around him, and longing once more to see his darling Bellissima, but he had not gone far before he was surrounded by four terrible sphinxes who would very soon have torn him to pieces with their sharp talons if it had not been for the Mermaid's diamond sword. For, no sooner had he flashed it before their eyes than down they fell at his feet quite helpless, and he killed them with one blow. But he had hardly turned to continue his search when he met six dragons covered with scales that were harder than iron. Frightful as this encounter was the King's courage was unshaken, and by the aid of his wonderful sword he cut them in pieces one after the other. Now he hoped his difficulties were over, but at the next turning, he was met by one which he did not know how to overcome. Four-and-twenty pretty and graceful nymphs advanced toward him, holding garlands of flowers, with which they barred the way.

'Where are you going, Prince?' they said; 'it is our duty to guard this place, and if we let you pass great misfortunes will happen to you and to us. We beg you not to insist upon going on. Do you want to kill four-and-twenty girls who have never displeased you in any way?'

The King did not know what to do or to say. It went against all his ideas as a knight to do anything a lady begged him not to do; but, as he hesitated, a voice in his ear said: 'Strike! Strike! And do not spare, or your Princess is lost forever!'

So, without reply to the nymphs, he rushed forward instantly, breaking their garlands, and scattering them in all directions; and then went on without further hindrance to the little wood where he had seen Bellissima. She was seated by the brook looking pale and weary when he reached her, and he would have thrown himself down at her feet, but she drew herself away from him with as much indignation as if he had been the Yellow Dwarf.

'Ah! Princess,' he cried, 'do not be angry with me. Let me explain everything. I am not faithless or to blame for what has happened. I am a miserable wretch who has displeased you without being able to help himself.'

'Ah!' cried Bellissima, 'did I not see you flying through the air with the loveliest being imaginable? Was that against your will?'

'Indeed it was, Princess,' he answered. 'The wicked Fairy of the Desert, not content with chaining me to a rock, carried me off in her chariot to the other end of the earth, where I should even now be a captive but for the unexpected help of a friendly mermaid, who brought me here to rescue you, my Princess, from the unworthy hands that hold you. Do not refuse the aid of your most faithful lover.'

So saying, he threw himself at her feet and held her by her robe. But, alas! In so doing he let fall the magic sword, and the Yellow Dwarf, who was crouching behind a lettuce, no sooner saw it than he sprang out and seized it, well knowing its wonderful power.

The Princess gave a cry of terror on seeing the Dwarf, but this only irritated the little monster; muttering a few magical words he summoned two giants, who bound the King with great chains of iron.

'Now,' said the Dwarf, 'I am master of my rival's fate, but I will give him his life and permission to depart unharmed if you, Princess, will consent to marry me.'

'Let me die a thousand times rather,' cried the unhappy King.

'Alas!' cried the Princess, 'must you die? Could anything be more terrible?'

'That you should marry that little wretch would be far more terrible,' answered the King.

'At least,' continued she, 'let us die together.'

'Let me have the satisfaction of dying for you, my Princess,' said he.

'Oh, no, no!' she cried, turning to the Dwarf; 'rather than that I will do as you wish.'

'Cruel Princess!' said the King, 'would you make my life horrible to me by marrying another before my eyes?'

'Not so,' replied the Yellow Dwarf; 'you are a rival of whom I am too much afraid; you shall not see our marriage.'

So saying, in spite of Bellissima's tears and cries, he stabbed the King to the heart with the diamond sword.

The poor Princess, seeing her lover lying dead at her feet, could no longer live without him; she sank down by him and died of a broken heart.

So ended these unfortunate lovers, whom not even the Mermaid could help, because all the magic power had been lost with the diamond sword.

As to the wicked Dwarf, he preferred to see the Princess dead rather than married to the King of the Gold Mines; and the Fairy of the Desert, when she heard of the King's adventures, pulled down the grand monument which she had built, and was so angry at the trick that had been played her that she hated him as much as she had loved him before.

The kind Mermaid, grieved at the sad fate of the lovers, caused them to be changed into two tall palm trees, which stand always side by side, whispering together of their faithful love and caressing one another with their interlacing branches.

From: The Blue Fairy Book

The Two Jugglers

One beautiful spring day two men strolled into the public square of a well-known Chinese city. They were plainly dressed and looked like ordinary countrymen who had come in to see the sights. Judging by their faces, they were father and son. The elder, a wrinkled man of perhaps fifty, wore a scant grey beard. The younger had a small box on his shoulder.

At the hour when these strangers entered the public square, a large crowd had gathered, for it was a feast day, and everyone was bent on having a good time. All the people seemed very happy. Some, seated in little open-air booths, were eating, drinking, and smoking. Others were buying odds and ends from the street vendors, tossing coins, and playing various games of chance.

The two men walked about aimlessly. They seemed to have no friends among the pleasure-seekers. At last, however, as they stood reading a public notice posted at the entrance of the town hall or yamen, a bystander asked them who they were.

'Oh, we are jugglers from a distant province,' said the elder, smiling and pointing towards the box. 'We can do many tricks for the amusement of the people.'

Soon it was spread about among the crowd that two famous jugglers had just arrived from the capital, and that they were able to perform many wonderful deeds. Now it happened that the mayor of the city, at that very moment, was entertaining a number of guests in the yamen. They had just finished eating, and the host was wondering what he should do to amuse his friends when a servant told him of the jugglers.

'Ask them what they can do,' said the mayor eagerly. 'I will pay them well if they can really amuse us, but I want something more than the old tricks of knife-throwing and balancing. They must show us something new.'

The servant went outside and spoke to the jugglers: 'The great man bids you tell him what you can do. If you can amuse his visitors he will bring them out to the private grandstand, and let you perform before them and the people who are gathered together.'

'Tell your honourable master,' said the elder, whom we shall call Chang, 'that, try us as he will, he will not be disappointed. Tell him that we come from the unknown land of dreams and visions, that we can turn rocks into mountains, rivers into oceans, mice into elephants, in short, that there is nothing in magic too difficult for us to do.'

The official was delighted when he heard the report of his servant. 'Now we may have a little fun,' he said to his guests, 'for there are jugglers outside who will perform their wonderful tricks before us.'

The guests filed out onto the grandstand at one side of the public square. The mayor commanded that a rope should be stretched across so as to leave an open space in full view of the crowd, where the two jugglers might give their exhibition.

For a time, the two strangers entertained the people with some of the simpler tricks, such as spinning plates in the air, tossing bowls up and catching them on chopsticks, making flowers grow from empty pots, and transforming one object into another. At last, however, the mayor cried out: 'These tricks are very good of their kind, but how about those idle boasts of changing rivers into oceans and mice into elephants? Did you not say that you came from the land of dreams? These tricks you have done are stale and shop-worn. Have you nothing new with which to regale my guests on this holiday?'

'Most certainly, your excellency. But surely you would not have a labourer do more than his employer requires? Would that not be quite contrary to the teachings of our fathers? Be assured, sir, anything that you demand I can do for you. Only say the word.'

The mayor laughed outright at this boasting language. 'Take care, my man! Do not go too far with your promises. There are too many impostors around for me to believe every stranger. Hark you! No lying, for if you lie in the presence of my guests, I shall take great pleasure in having you beaten.'

'My words are quite true, your excellency,' repeated the juggler earnestly. 'What have we to gain by deceit, we who have performed our miracles before the countless hosts of yonder Western Heaven?'

'Ha, ha! Hear the braggarts!' shouted the guests. 'What shall we command them to do?'

For a moment they consulted together, whispering and laughing.

'I have it,' cried the host finally. 'Our feast was short of fruit, since this is the off-season. Suppose we let this fellow supply us. Here, fellow, produce us a peach, and be quick about it. We have no time for fooling.'

'What, masters, a peach?' exclaimed the elder juggler in mock dismay. 'Surely at this season, you do not expect a peach.'

'Caught at his own game,' laughed the guests, and the people began to hoot derisively.

'But, father, you promised to do anything he required,' urged the son. 'If he asks even a peach, how can you refuse and at the same time save your face?'

'Hear the boy talk,' mumbled the father, 'and yet, perhaps he's right. Very well, masters,' turning to the crowd, 'if it's a peach you want, why, a peach you shall have, even though I must send into the garden of the Western Heaven for the fruit.'

The people became silent and the mayor's guests forgot to laugh. The old man, still muttering, opened the box from which he had been taking the magic bowls, plates, and other articles. 'To think of people wanting peaches at this season! What is the world coming to?'

After fumbling in the box for some moments he drew out a skein of golden thread, fine-spun and as light as gossamer. No sooner had he unwound a portion of this thread than a sudden gust of wind carried it up into the air above the heads of the onlookers. Faster and faster the old man paid out the magic coil, higher and higher the free end rose into the heavens, until, strain his eyes as he would, no one present could see into what far region it had vanished.

'Wonderful, wonderful!' shouted the people with one voice, 'the old man is a fairy.'

For a moment they forgot all about the mayor, the jugglers, and the peach, so amazed were they at beholding the flight of the magic thread.

At last, the old man seemed satisfied with the distance to which his cord had sailed, and, with a bow to the spectators, he tied the end to a large wooden pillar which helped to support the roof of the grandstand. For a moment the structure trembled and swayed as if it too would be carried off into the blue ether, the guests turned pale and clutched their chairs for support, but not even the mayor dared to speak, so sure were they now that they were in the presence of fairies.

'Everything is ready for the journey,' said old Chang calmly.

'What! Shall you leave us?' asked the mayor, finding his voice again.

'I? Oh, no, my old bones are not spry enough for quick climbing. My son here will bring us the magic peach. He is handsome and active enough to enter that heavenly garden. Graceful, oh graceful is that peach tree – of course, you remember the line from the poem – and a graceful man must pluck the fruit.'

The mayor was still more surprised at the juggler's knowledge of a famous poem from the classics. It made him and his friends all the more certain that the newcomers were indeed fairies.

The young man, at a sign from his father, tightened his belt and the bands about his ankles, and then, with a graceful gesture to the astonished people, sprang upon the magic string, balanced himself for a moment on the steep incline, and then ran as nimbly up as a sailor would have mounted a rope ladder. Higher and higher he climbed till he seemed no bigger than a lark ascending into the blue sky, and then, like some tiny speck, far, far away, on the western horizon.

The people gazed in open-mouthed wonder. They were struck dumb and filled with some nameless fear; they hardly dared to look at the enchanter who stood calmly in their midst, smoking his long-stemmed pipe.

The mayor, ashamed of having laughed at and threatened this man who was clearly a fairy, did not know what to say. He snapped his long fingernails and looked at his guests in mute astonishment. The visitors silently drank their tea, and the crowd of sightseers craned their necks in a vain effort to catch sight of the vanished fairy. Only one in all that assembly, a bright-eyed little boy of eight, dared to break the silence, and he caused a hearty burst of merriment by crying out, 'Oh, daddy, will the bad young man fly off into the sky and leave his poor father all alone?'

The greybeard laughed loudly with the others and tossed the lad a copper. 'Ah, the good boy,' he said smiling, 'he has been well trained to love his father; no fear of foreign ways spoiling his filial piety.'

After a few moments of waiting, old Chang laid aside his pipe and fixed his eyes once more on the western sky. 'It is coming,' he said quietly. 'The peach will soon be here.'

Suddenly he held out his hand as if to catch some falling object, but, look as they would, the people could see nothing. Swish! Thud! It came like a streak of light, and, lo, there in the magician's fingers was a peach, the most beautiful specimen the people had ever seen, large and rosy.

'Straight from the garden of the gods,' said the juggler, handing the fruit to the mayor, 'a peach in the Second Moon, and the snow hardly off the ground.'

'HIGHER AND HIGHER HE CLIMBED.'

Trembling with excitement, the official took the peach and cut it open. It was large enough for all his guests to have a taste, and such a taste it was! They smacked their lips and wished for more, secretly thinking that never again would ordinary fruit be worth the eating.

But all this time the old juggler, magician, fairy or whatever you choose to call him, was looking anxiously into the sky. The result of this trick was more than he had bargained for. True, he had been able to produce the magic peach which the mayor had called for, but his son, where was his son? He shaded his eyes and looked far up into the blue heavens, and so did the people, but no one could catch a glimpse of the departed youth.

'Oh, my son, my son,' cried the old man in despair, 'how cruel is the fate that has robbed me of you, the only prop of my declining years! Oh, my boy, my boy, would that I had not sent you on so perilous a journey! Who now will look after my grave when I am gone?'

Suddenly the silken cord on which the young man had sped so daringly into the sky, gave a quick jerk which almost toppled over the post to which it was tied, and there, before the very eyes of the people, it fell from the lofty height, a silken pile on the ground in front of them.

The greybeard uttered a loud cry and covered his face with his hands.

'Alas! The whole story is plain enough,' he sobbed.

'My boy was caught in the act of plucking the magic peach from the garden of the gods, and they have thrown him into prison. Woe is me! Ah! Woe is me!'

The mayor and his friends were deeply touched by the old man's grief, and tried in vain to comfort him.

'Perhaps he will return,' they said. 'Have courage!'

'Yes, but in what a shape?' replied the magician. 'See! Even now they are restoring him to his father.'

The people looked, and they saw twirling and twisting through the air the young man's arm. It fell upon the ground in front of them at the fairy's feet. Next came the head, a leg, the body. One by one before the gasping, shuddering people, the parts of the unfortunate young man were restored to his father.

After the first outburst of wild, frantic grief the old man by a great effort gained control of his feelings and began to gather up these parts, putting them tenderly into the wooden box.

By this time many of the spectators were weeping at the sight of the father's affliction.

'Come,' said the mayor at last, deeply moved, 'let us present the old man with sufficient money to give his boy a decent burial.'

All present agreed willingly, for there is no sight in China that causes greater pity than that of an aged parent robbed by death of an only son. The copper cash fell in a shower at the juggler's feet, and soon tears of gratitude were mingled with those of sorrow. He gathered up the money and tied it in a large black cloth. Then a wonderful change came over his face. He seemed all of a sudden to forget his grief. Turning to the box, he raised the lid. The people heard him say:

'Come, my son; the crowd is waiting for you to thank them. Hurry up! They have been very kind to us.'

In an instant, the box was thrown open with a bang, and before the mayor and his friends, before the eyes of all the sightseers the young man, strong and whole once more, stepped forth and bowed, clasping his hands and giving the national salute.

For a moment all were silent. Then, as the wonder of the whole thing dawned upon them, the people broke forth into a tumult of shouts, laughter, and compliments.

'The fairies have surely come to visit us!' they shouted.

'The city will be blessed with good fortune! Perhaps it is Fairy Old Boy himself who is among us!'

The mayor rose and addressed the jugglers, thanking them in the name of the city for their visit and for the taste they had given to him and his guests of the peach from the heavenly orchard.

Even as he spoke, the magic box opened again; the two fairies disappeared inside, the lid closed, and the chest rose from the ground above the heads of the people. For a moment it floated around in a circle like some homing pigeon trying to find its bearings before starting on a return journey. Then, with a sudden burst of speed, it shot off into the heavens and vanished from the sight of those below, and not a thing remained as proof of the strange visitors except the magic peach seed that lay beside the teacups on the mayor's table.

According to the most ancient writings, there is now nothing left to tell of this story. It has been declared, however, by later scholars that the official and his friends who had eaten the magic peach, at once began to feel a change in their lives. While, before the coming of the fairies, they had lived unfairly, accepting bribes and taking part in many shameful practices, now, after tasting of the heavenly fruit, they began to grow better. The people soon began to honour and love them, saying, 'Surely these great men are not like others of their kind, for these men are just and honest in their dealings with us. They seem not to be ruling for their own reward!'

However, this may be, we do know that before many years their city became the centre of the greatest peach-growing section of China, and even yet when strangers walk in the orchards and look up admiringly at the beautiful sweet-smelling fruit, the natives sometimes ask proudly, 'And have you never heard about the wonderful peach which was the beginning of all our orchards, the magic peach the fairies brought us from the Western Heaven?'

From: A Chinese Wonder Book

The Princess of the Springs

ONCE, LONG AGO, the Moon Giant wooed the beautiful giantess who dwells in the Great River and won her love. He built for her a wonderful palace where the Great River runs into the sea. It was made of mother-of-pearl with rich carvings, and gold and silver and precious stones were used to adorn it. Never before in all the world had a giant or giantess possessed such a magnificent home.

When the baby daughter of the Moon Giant and the Giantess of the Great River was born it was decreed among the giants that she should be the Princess of all the Springs and should rule over all the rivers and lakes. The light of her eyes was like the moonbeams, and her smile was like moonlight on still waters. Her strength was as the strength of the Great River, and the fleetness of her foot was as the swiftness of the Great River.

As the beautiful Spring Princess grew older, many suitors came to sing her praises beneath the palace windows, but she favoured none of them. She was so happy living in her own lovely palace with her own dear mother that she did not care at all for any suitor. No other daughter ever loved her mother as the Spring Princess loved the Giantess of the Great River.

At last, the Sun Giant came to woo the Spring Princess. The strength of the Sun Giant was as the strength of ten of the other suitors of the fair princess. He was so powerful that he won her heart.

When he asked her to marry him, however, and go with him to his own palace, the Spring Princess shook her lovely head.

'O Sun Giant, you are so wonderful and so powerful that I love you as I never before have loved a suitor who sang beneath my palace window,' said she, 'but I love my mother, too. I cannot go away with you and leave my own dear mother. It would break my heart.'

The Sun Giant told the Spring Princess again and again of his great love for her, of his magnificent palace which would be her new home, of the happy life which awaited her as queen of the palace. At length she listened to his pleadings and decided that she could leave home and live with him for nine months of the year. For three months of every year, however, she would have to return to the wonderful palace of mother-of-pearl where the Great River runs into the sea and spend the time with her mother, the Giantess of the Great River.

The Sun Giant at last sorrowfully consented to this arrangement and the wedding feast was held. It lasted for seven days and seven nights. Then the Spring Princess went away with the Sun Giant to his own home.

Every year the Spring Princess went to visit her mother for three months according to the agreement. For three months of every year she lived in the palace of mother-of-pearl where the Great River runs into the sea. For three months of every year, the rivers sang once more as they rushed along their way. For three months the lakes sparkled in the bright sunlight as their hearts once more were brimful of joy.

When at last the little son of the Spring Princess was born she wanted to take him with her when she went to visit her mother. The Sun Giant, however, did not approve of such a plan. He firmly refused to allow the child to leave home. After much pleading, all in vain, the Spring Princess set out upon her journey alone, with sorrow in her heart. She left her baby son with the best nurses she could procure.

Now it happened that the Giantess of the Great River had not expected that her daughter would be able to visit her that year. She had thought that all the rivers and lakes, the palace of mother-of-pearl, and her own mother heart would have to get along as best they could without a visit from the Spring Princess. The Giantess of the Great River had gone away to water the earth. One of the land giants had taken her prisoner and would not let her escape.

When the Spring Princess arrived at the beautiful palace of mother-of-pearl and gold and silver and precious stones, where the Great River runs into the sea, there was no one at home. She ran from room to room in the palace calling out, 'O dear mother, Giantess of the Great River, dear, dear mother! Where are you? Where have you hidden yourself?'

There was no answer. Her own voice echoed back to her through the beautiful halls of mother-of-pearl with their rich carvings. The palace was entirely deserted.

She ran outside the palace and called to the fishes of the river, 'O fishes of the river, have you seen my own dear mother?'

She called to the sands of the sea, 'O sands of the sea, have you seen my darling mother?'

She called to the shells of the shore, 'O shells of the shore, have you seen my precious mother?'

There was no answer. No one knew what had become of the Giantess of the Great River.

The Spring Princess was so worried that she thought her heart would break in its anguish. In her distress, she ran over all the earth.

Then she went to the house of the Great Wind. The Giant of the Great Wind was away, but his old father was at home. He was very sorry for the Spring Princess when he heard her sad story.

'I am sure my son can help you find your mother,' he said as he comforted her.

'He will soon get home from his day's work.'

When the Giant of the Great Wind reached home he was in a terrible temper. He stormed and raged and gave harsh blows to everything he met. His father had hid the Spring Princess in a closet out of the way, and it was fortunate indeed for her that he had done so.

After the Great Wind Giant had taken his bath and eaten his dinner he was better-natured. Then his father said to him, 'O my son, if a wandering princess had come this way on purpose to ask you a question, what would you do to her?'

'Why, I'd answer her question as best I could, of course,' responded the Giant of the Great Wind.

His father straightway opened the closet door and the Spring Princess stepped out. In spite of her long wanderings and great anguish of mind she was still very lovely as she knelt before the Giant of the Great Wind in her soft silvery green garments embroidered with pearls and diamonds. The big heart of the Giant of the Great Wind was touched at her beauty and at her grief.

'O Giant of the Great Wind,' said the Spring Princess, as he gently raised her from her knees before him, 'I am the daughter of the Giantess of the Great River. I have lost my mother. I have searched for her through all the earth and now I have come to you for help. Can you tell me anything about where she is and how I can find her?'

The Giant of the Great Wind put on his thinking cap. He thought hard.

'Your mother is in the power of a land giant who has imprisoned her,' he said. 'I happen to know all about the affair. I passed that way only yesterday. I'll gladly go with you and help you get her home. We'll start at once.'

The Giant of the Great Wind took the Spring Princess back to earth on his swift horses. Then he stormed the castle of the land giant who had imprisoned the Giantess of the Great River. The Spring Princess dug quietly beneath the castle walls to the dungeon where her mother was confined. You may be sure that her mother was overjoyed to see her.

When the Spring Princess had led her mother safely outside the castle walls she thanked the Giant of the Great Wind for all he had done to help her. Then the Giantess of the Great River and the Spring Princess hastened back to the wonderful palace of mother-of-pearl set with gold and silver and precious stones, where the Great River runs into the Sea. As soon as she had safely reached there once more the Spring Princess suddenly remembered that she had stayed away from her home in the palace of the Sun Giant longer than the three months she was supposed to stay according to the agreement. She at once said goodbye to her mother and hastened to the home of the Sun Giant, her husband, and to her baby son.

Now the Sun Giant had been very much worried at first when the three months had passed and the Spring Princess had not come back to him and her little son. Then he became angry. He became so angry that he married another princess. The new wife discharged the nurses who were taking care of the tiny son of the Spring Princess and put him in the kitchen just as if he had been a poor woman's baby.

When the Spring Princess arrived at the palace of the Sun Giant the very first person she saw was her own little son, so dirty and neglected that she hardly recognized him. Then she found out all that had happened in her absence.

The Spring Princess quickly seized her child and clasped him tight in her arms. Then she fled to the depths of the sea and wept, and wept, and wept. The waters of the sea rose so high that they reached even to the palace of the Sun Giant. They covered the palace, and the Sun Giant, his new wife, and all the court entirely disappeared from view. For forty days the face of the Sun Giant was not seen upon the earth.

The little son of the Spring Princess grew up to be the Giant of the Rain. In the rainy season and the season of thunder showers he rules upon the earth. He sends upon the earth such tears as the Spring Princess shed in the depths of the seas.

From: Tales of Giants from Brazil

The Boy Who Set a Snare for the Sun

At the time when the animals reigned in the earth, they had killed all the people but a girl and her little brother, and these two were living in fear, in an out-of-the-way place. The boy was very small, and never grew beyond the size of a mere infant; but the girl increased with her years, so that the task of providing food and shelter fell wholly upon her. She went out daily to get wood for the lodge fire, and she took her little brother with her that no mishap might befall him; for he was too little to leave alone. A big bird, of a mischievous disposition, might have flown away with him. She made him a bow and arrows, and said to him one day, 'My little brother, I will leave you behind where I have been gathering the wood; you must hide yourself, and you will soon see the snow-birds come and pick the worms out of the logs which I have piled up. Shoot one of them and bring it home.'

He obeyed her, and tried his best to kill one, but he came home unsuccessful. His sister told him that he must not despair, but try again the next day.

She accordingly left him at the gathering place of the wood, and returned to the lodge. Toward night-fall, she heard his little footsteps crackling through the snow, and he hurried in and threw down, with an air of triumph, one of the birds which he had killed.

'My sister,' said he, 'I wish you to skin it, and stretch the skin, and when I have killed more, I will have a coat made out of them.'

'But what shall we do with the body?' said she; for they had always up to that time lived upon greens and berries.

'Cut it in two,' he answered, 'and season our pottage with one half of it at a time.'

It was their first dish of game, and they relished it greatly.

The boy kept on in his efforts, and in the course of time he killed ten birds – out of the skins of which his sister made him a little coat: being very small, he had a very pretty coat, and a bird skin to spare.

'Sister,' said he, one day, as he paraded up and down before the lodge, enjoying his new coat, and fancifying himself the greatest little fellow in the world – as he was, for there was no other beside him – 'My sister, are we really alone in the world, or are we playing at it? Is there nobody else living? And, tell me, was all this great broad earth and this huge big sky made for a little boy and girl like you and me?'

She told him, by no means; there were many folks very unlike a harmless girl and boy, such as they were, who lived in a certain other quarter of the earth, who had killed off all of their kinsfolk; and that if he would live blameless and not endanger his life, he must never go where they were. This only served to inflame the boy's curiosity; and he soon after took his bow and arrows and went in that direction. After walking a long time and meeting no one, he became tired, and stretched himself upon a high green knoll where the day's warmth had melted off the snow.

It was a charming place to lie upon, and he fell asleep; and, while sleeping, the sun beat so hot upon him that it not only singed his bird-skin coat, but it so shrivelled and shrunk and tightened it upon the little boy's body, as to wake him up.

When he felt how the sun had seared and the mischief its fiery beams had played with the coat he was so proud of, he flew into a great passion, and berated the sun in a terrible way for a little boy no higher than a man's knee, and he vowed fearful things against it.

'Do not think you are too high,' said he; 'I shall revenge myself. Oh, sun! I will have you for a plaything yet.'

On coming home, he gave an account of his misfortune to his sister, and bitterly bewailed the spoiling of his new coat. He would not eat – not so much as a single berry. He lay down as one that fasts; nor did he move nor change his manner of lying for ten full days, though his sister strove to prevail on him to rise. At the end of ten days, he turned over, and then he lay full ten days on the other side.

When he got up he was very pale, but very resolute too. He bade his sister make a snare, for, he informed her, that he meant to catch the sun. She said she had nothing; but after a while she brought forward a deer's sinew which the father had left, and which she soon made into a string suitable for a noose. The moment she showed it to him he was quite wroth, and told her that would not do, and directed her to find something else. She said she had nothing – nothing at all.

At last, she thought of the bird-skin that was left over when the coat was made; and this she wrought into a string. With this, the little boy was more vexed than before.

'The sun has had enough of my bird-skins,' he said; 'find something else.'

She went out of the lodge saying to herself,

'Was there ever so obstinate a boy?' She did not dare to answer this time that she had nothing. Luckily she thought of her own beautiful hair, and pulling some of it from among her locks, she quickly braided it into a cord, and, returning, she handed it to her brother. The moment his eye fell upon this jet-black braid he was delighted.

'This will do,' he said; and he immediately began to run it back and forth through his hands as swiftly as he could; and as he drew it forth, he tried its strength. He said again, 'this will do;' and winding it in a glossy coil about his shoulders, he set out a little after midnight. His object was to catch the sun before he rose. He fixed his snare firmly on a spot just where the sun must strike the land as it rose above the earth; and sure enough, he caught the sun, so that it was held fast in the cord and did not rise.

The animals who ruled the earth were immediately put into great commotion. They had no light; and they ran to and fro, calling out to each other, and inquiring what had happened. They summoned a council to debate upon the matter, and an old dormouse, suspecting where the trouble lay, proposed that someone should be appointed to go and cut the cord. This was a bold thing to undertake, as the rays of the sun could not fail to burn whoever should venture so near to them.

At last the venerable dormouse himself undertook it, for the very good reason that no one else would. At this time the dormouse was the largest animal in the world. When he stood up he looked like a mountain. It made haste to the place where the sun lay ensnared, and as it came nearer and nearer, its back began to smoke and burn with the heat, and the whole top of his huge bulk was turned in a very short time to enormous heaps of ashes. It succeeded, however, in cutting the cord with its teeth and freeing the sun, which rolled up again, as round and beautiful as ever, into the wide blue sky. But the dormouse - or blind woman as it is called - was shrunk away to a very small size; and that is the reason why it is now one of the tiniest creatures upon the earth.

The little boy returned home when he discovered that the sun had escaped his snare, and devoted himself entirely to hunting.

'If the beautiful hair of my sister would not hold the sun fast, nothing in the world could,' he said.

'He was not born, a little fellow like himself, to look after the sun. It required one greater and wiser than he was to regulate that.'

And he went out and shot ten more snowbirds; for in this business he was very expert; and he had a new bird-skin coat made, which was prettier than the one he had worn before.

From: The Indian Fairy Book

Finis

Workbooks From The Scheherazade Foundation

We hope that you have enjoyed this collection of stories, gleaned from varying cultural corners of the world, and that you have been entertained by them.

But, have you considered the deeper meanings and interwoven layers that lie hidden beneath the surface?

At The Scheherazade Foundation, we believe that Teaching-Stories contain wisdom, information, and marvels that have the power to transform the way we think, and thereby change our lives.

Employed as a bedrock of culture throughout the centuries – challenging established patterns of thinking, while passing on knowledge and values – tales such as the ones contained in this volume are a rich resource ready and waiting to be mined.

As an aid to help in the perception of less-obvious facets and layers, we have created a series of original Workbooks. Aimed at stimulating thought-provoking discussions and igniting deep reflection, these tools will assist in unlocking the power of Teaching-Stories.

www.ingramcontent.com/pod-product-compliance
Lightning Source LLC
Chambersburg PA
CBHW030611310726
48979CB00003B/662
* 9 7 8 1 9 1 5 3 1 1 1 2 2 *